Right
Villain

TITLES BY JAY GEE HEATH

ISBN eBook 978-0-9992454-6-0
ISBN Print Book 978-0-9992454-7-7
Library of Congress Control Number: 2021903481
Naples, Florida

Email the author at jaygeeheath@gmail.com

Visit her webpage at http://www.jaygeeheath.com/

Right Villain

jay gee heath

DEDICATION

Sam again

He is always here to encourage.

THE SAME CREW!!!!

Thanks to
Janet Benjamins
Jean Smith
JoAnne Sullivan
Lisa Wroble

MONDAY

Annie couldn't put it off any longer. She had to tell them he was coming. For ten years she'd kept Chris private. To herself. Hadn't shared him. Sure, the kids—the Gang of Five they called themselves—knew she had a guy, but they didn't know anything else. And Chris knew about the Gang, because she had shared their names, their successes. She'd shared good news with him and some of the missteps. But now her two worlds were about to collide. Not just meet but intermingle. Damn.

Get over it, she told herself. She wanted Chris to meet her kids and he'd be meeting them in a few hours when he flew into Bear. So really, it was a good thing. She should be happy. She was happy. Except the kids didn't know he was coming. And Becca meeting Chris? Always would have been dicey. But in the middle of this situation? That was the Problem. With a capital P.

She looked at the text again hoping maybe she'd misread it. Hoping it said he'd arrive at nine on the eleventh, not eleven on the ninth. Hadn't changed. Wasn't going to change. Still said he'd be at the airport today at eleven, in an hour, just enough time to drive there. And she hadn't told him about the current complications. There was no reason to. Yeah, keep telling yourself that, she thought.

So, she had to tell them. Now. And it wasn't going to make them happy.

Gibbs, Becca, Kevin, and Daffy were watching her. Waiting. She licked her upper lip. She looked at the text again. Fidgeted. Damn. She hated people who fidgeted. But as soon as she told them, she would lose control. And that made her fidget. Loss of control made her angry and edgy. Edgy made her fidget. She squeezed her lips together for control. Fake control. Opened her mouth to speak. Couldn't seem to find her voice. That made her angry all over again.

She'd never been at a loss for words. And with this group that was an accomplishment. Spit it out girl, she told herself. Say it. Tell them.

"I have a complication," she said. Complication? Really, Annie? That was the best she could do? Well, it was sort of a complication. Still, it sounded stupid. Should she have said confession? She shoved her hands in her pockets to keep them still. The right hand wrapped around her cell with the text.

"What type of complication?" Becca asked. Becca, not part of the original Gang of Five. Becca would have made it Gang of Six, or would that be eight if you counted the Boys. But they hadn't changed the name. The original five had saved themselves and together had rescued The Boys and Becca.

"I have a friend visiting." Annie paused and added. "Today."

Becca flicked her hand. "So, call her and tell her you're sick."

Annie shook her head. "Can't. My friend is flying in."

"You have a friend flying in today and you are just telling us now?" Becca let the annoyance leak through.

Annie ignored the tone; Becca had a right to be annoyed. "Yes," she replied gruffly. Never display weakness.

Ryan asked, "When today?" Skipping to the critical fact.

Annie grimaced and pulled out her cell, looked at it, fidgeted. Damn. "An hour"

Becca reached for Annie's cell. "Let me see that."

Annie shoved it back in her pocket. She couldn't let Becca read the full text, the part where Chris said he missed her hands all over him.

2

Becca eyed her a moment, thinking, then morphed into her cop mode, leaned forward, threatening. Annie almost took a step back but stood firm. Never back up. Becca didn't intimidate her. Becca might be a cop, ex-cop, but Annie had helped raise her and wasn't cowed.

Daffy moved. He'd been leaning against the counter, but now he walked over to the coffee pot and refilled his cup, distracting everyone for a moment. He smiled at the interplay. Not much phased him, and as tough as Becca was, he'd put his money on Annie.

Ryan placed a soothing hand on Becca's shoulder to calm her and asked, "Are you meeting her at the airport? In town? For lunch? What's the plan?"

Annie straightened to her full height and said, "I'm meeting *him* at the airport. In an hour."

The male pronoun got Becca's full attention and she absently patted her husband's hand, her annoyance replaced by speculation.

Just what Annie hadn't wanted. God, she hadn't wanted them to know about Chris, which was why she'd left it so late.

"Him, then," Ryan said. "Is he in the air already? Maybe you can reach him before he boards?"

"Um. No. I tried. He has his cell off."

"Which airport?" They were close to an assortment of airports, all different sizes.

"New Castle." It was a small, friendly airfield, about a half hour away. Yes, she'd put it off as long as she could.

"And you are going to meet him there in an hour." Gibbs looked at his watch.

She nodded.

"That gives us a little time."

"Can one of us meet him?" Ryan asked and then answered his own question. "No. You need to meet him." He scratched his head. "When he gets here, what were you planning? He stays in town? You go to, um, visit?"

Annie pressed her lips together and felt her face warm and knew she was turning pink, a pale shade she hoped. What she was going to do with Chris was her personal business. "That was the plan, yes. I go to town to visit." She didn't hesitate before the word visit but saw Becca's eyes widen. "I'll do whatever works best for you. I don't have to see him. I can send him a text."

Ryan held up a hand. "Give me a minute here. Sit and be quiet."

She didn't want to sit. She wanted to pace. Or hit something. She wanted to blame someone. Sure, she could blame Prowitt, for sending those goons after her. Or Cav and Ryan for not catching Prowitt or his goons. But it was all her fault. She had no one to blame except herself.

Daffy passed her a cup of coffee, took a sip of his own. Kevin, the only one here from the original gang, waited. Quiet. Not like him at all, but then he was in almost the same position as Annie. Because Annie had taken her complication to him. Not that it had been a problem then.

Ryan would find a solution to her 'complication'.

"We don't want you going to town alone, Annie. You'll be too vulnerable. Prowitt's people will be looking for you."

"I don't have to go. I can text Chris. Tell him I can't meet him. He'll get the message when he lands."

"Tell me what kind of man is he? Will he leave if you ask? Get on the first plane out? Give me a feel for the guy."

Annie looked at them. Her friends. FBI Agent Ryan Gibbs, his wife, ex-cop Becca, Daffy, a bodyguard, her bodyguard right now, married to Penney, one of The Gang. She shook her head. "No. He won't leave. Whether I tell him to or not. Especially, he won't leave if he thinks I'm in trouble. He's worked in remote wilderness areas for the last ten years and has dealt with all types of emergencies and disasters. He's smart and tough. He won't leave."

"What were you planning to do while he was here?" Ryan asked, adding quickly, "in general."

She realized he thought that what they planned to do would involve bedrooms and hot sex. Which it did. "Spend time together, hang out. Take stock. He's at a crossroads. That's what the visit is for. To decide his future." Normally they met far away from Bear, but this time was different. This time, he said he was staying. Done with travel and remote area adventures. She wasn't so sure.

"How much can we tell him?" Ryan asked and again answered his own question. "All of it. He needs to know what is happening before he can decide to stay. Maybe you both should fly out."

"No. I'm not leaving," Annie said adamantly.

Ryan nodded once. "Where is he going to stay? I don't want you staying in town with him and I don't want you going back and forth. You'll be too vulnerable. You stay here."

She pressed her lips together getting ready to disagree.

"Is it okay with you, if he stays here?" Ryan asked her. "Here in the gatehouse or up at the main house."

"Um." She shrugged. "Sure." She looked at Kevin, it was his house.

He shrugged. "Here in the gatehouse? Or up at the main house? You say the word Annie. Whatever you want."

"Main house. With me. In my quarters." As she spoke, Annie stared Becca in the eye. "With me," she repeated. Nothing to be ashamed of and she wasn't surprised when Becca's curiosity replaced her annoyance.

"This is him, isn't it? This is your guy? The man you don't ever talk about."

"Yes, this is my guy, and I am still not talking about him. And you will behave yourself. You will not interrogate him, Rebecca Anne Travis." Becca might be a cop, but Annie was still the authority figure in the family.

"I'll try to be good," Becca promised, but she didn't look like she intended to keep that promise. Interrogation was bred into her. She'd be the first to question Chris. Be the spokesperson. Spokesman,

Annie corrected herself. Not spokesperson. Not spokeswoman. None of those effeminate, diminutive, politically correct titles for Becca. She'd be grilling Chris the minute he stepped in the door. But Chris was tough and could handle her. She hoped.

Becca did a happy dance. "We get to meet him. We're finally going to meet Annie's guy. Finally, after ten years. Chill the champagne." Becca paused in her happy dance. "Wait a minute. You left something out."

"Yes. I did. I left out quite a lot. Personal things which you don't need to know, Rebecca Anne," Annie said.

"His name, Annie. What's his name? Do you think you could tell us his name? You can share that personal information, can't you? Or we can just call him Annie's boyfriend or Lover Boy. Hmm, now that I think of it, I am kind of partial to Lover Boy."

She stopped and laughed when Annie turned the eye on her again. Put up her hands. "I'll call him Mister Lover Boy, Annie," she said respectfully with a smile.

"Christopher Nicolles, with two ells."

Becca reached for her tablet and began tapping.

Should have expected that, Annie thought. The Gang was a family of geeks, nerds. "Chris isn't on any social media sites. Some of his articles are online and you might find them. You'd enjoy them. He has a unique style of writing which makes dry, esoteric, scientific studies both interesting and understandable." She didn't mention Chris's book was even better.

"How do you communicate?" Ryan asked motioning toward her cell. "Text and calls?"

"Depends. Kevin has made sure my cell is secure and he gave me an app to send to Chris. But we generally use an email account under a bogus name. Kevin set it up for us. One of us will type an email, save it as a draft. The other one reads and deletes. We don't actually email anything. Certainly, nothing private and the account is totally encrypted. I have been around this gang long enough to learn some basic rules."

"Kevin set up an account for you? He knows Chris?" Becca complained.

Ryan patted Becca's shoulder gently and Annie replied, "No, Becca. I asked him how to set up a secure account. I didn't tell him what it was for or why I wanted it. He just assumed I'm as anal as the rest of you and said I should have been using it all along."

Ryan nodded. "Okay, probably doesn't make any difference in this case. Here's what we do. Daffy and I will go to the airport with you. You meet Chris, take him for a drink, give him a short-hand version. If he decides to stay, fine. If he doesn't, no harm done. Okay?" Ryan asked.

She nodded.

"If he decides to leave and take you with him, we'll put a couple of guards on you both. Discreetly."

Annie didn't like that. "I'm not running."

"We'll take it one step at a time," Ryan said. He checked his watch. "We leave now. Gives us a few minutes to check out the area."

They left immediately. She was nervous and scared as she drove to the airfield. Prowitt was a scary guy. Her stomach was in jitters and she checked her rear-view mirror frequently. Daffy was back there, but like Ryan ahead of her, she couldn't spot him. Ryan had told her she wouldn't see them.

She would tell Chris to go but she knew he wouldn't. Chris would stay, no doubt in her mind. There was no way he would leave once he knew she was in trouble. She hadn't convinced Ryan and Daffy. Ryan still hoped she would leave with Chris.

She couldn't see any end to the threat. Until they found Prowitt and arrested him, he would always be after her, watching, waiting. All because a little girl wore an armband. Annie shrugged it off, she couldn't go back and not recognize the bracelet or not act on that recognition. Wouldn't, even if she could.

When she arrived at the airport, she followed Daffy's instructions and backed into a parking spot in the small outdoor lot. She saw Daffy. Knew she wasn't supposed to look at him, but she couldn't help herself. He frowned and shook his head and she walked toward the only gate, checking her watch. The plane was rolling in early. Chris was never part of the immediate rush, he was normally one of the last off the plane. She hadn't told Daffy that, and the thought made her look toward him and away quickly. And then she saw Chris and forgot everything as her heart rolled over and lost a beat.

Despite the circumstances, she was eager to see him. This separation had been a long four months, in fact, each tour seemed longer. Was it because she was older? Lonely, maybe? Because the Gang were all on their own now, so she had more free time? Less responsibility?

She shook her head. Whatever the reason, it didn't matter. He was here. And she wanted him, wanted to touch him, wanted the comfort and support she got from him. Like Becca got from Ryan.

She'd tell Chris about Prowitt and then she'd take him home. She drank him in. His curly brown hair was mussed as usual around his craggy face which had a wide smile and the biggest darkest eyes. He had a winter parka and briefcase hanging over his shoulder. His white shirt sleeves were rolled up, displaying the red and gold dragon climbing his arm wrapped around the word, Annie. She stopped herself from jumping up and down and glanced once again at Daffy, who nodded encouragement. She hurried over to Chris and hugged him close. Breathed him in, held him tight. "Oh, it is so good to see you. Hold you," she whispered into his shoulder.

"Me too. Missed you. Missed you so much. Every day," he said. God it felt good to have her in his arms finally. Pressed against his body. She'd greeted him like she always did after a tour. Hungry for his touch. For him. He put a finger under her chin and lifted her face up. Just looked at her, his heart full. He kissed her. Not long and hard. Not how he wanted. That would have to wait, but enough to show her how he felt.

This tour had been hell. He'd marked every day off his calendar. A first for him. Every day crossed off was one day closer to coming home to Annie. To his future. Sure, the penguins had been fun. He'd worked with the Brits tracking breeding pairs by satellite transmitters. And he'd filled in as interim chopper pilot. The best of both worlds. The way he looked at it, they paid him to play. But he was done with travel, adventure, seeing the world. He was ready to put down roots. In Bear. With Annie. This would be his adventure, life here. With her if she was ready. Near her if she wasn't. He wasn't leaving her again. He smiled down at her. "Come-on, let's go get my duffle and head for that hotel room."

But she didn't move. Didn't smile back. And her eyes shifted. To the side. To a man at the back of the waiting area. She seemed to take comfort from his slight nod.

She'd brought a man with her? Why would she do that?

She said in a whisper, "We need to talk."

Oh oh. Nothing good ever happened after a lover said we need to talk. Especially with a man at the back of the room watching. No. No. she couldn't have fallen for another guy.

"About?" he asked.

She avoided the question, didn't answer, instead said, "Let's get a drink."

He didn't want to get a drink. He didn't want to talk. If she was going to tell him there was another man, she could do it now, here. He wasn't going to sit and have a friendly drink. But he followed her into the small cafe. "Is it another man?" he asked.

"Why would you ask that?" she asked, turning, surprised.

"Why wouldn't I? You came with another man to pick me up," he said as they selected a table in the dark corner of the coffee shop. A long, narrow room. A breakfast bar down the length. Five tables squeezed in.

"No. No I didn't."

"Then who is that guy?"

"What guy?" She glanced back nervously at that guy.

"That guy who's not watching you. Over there. The one at the counter. The one who followed us in here. The one you keep looking to for support." The one watching her in the mirror.

She couldn't have fallen for someone else. He knew that. It wasn't possible. Annie loved him. She'd always loved him.

"Annie. Just tell me." He took a deep breath. Forced the issue. "Just tell me. If you want to break it off, tell me. We don't have to have a drink. You can tell me now and leave with your boyfriend." He hated saying that and was surprised he could. And surprised at how much it hurt. Like a knife in his heart. Annie never dithered. Never equivocated. Never lied. She would tell him; he had left her too long. Tell him she had met another guy. After all this time, she was going to dump him.

He decided he wasn't going to let her go without a fight. He loved her. He wasn't letting her go now. He clenched his fingers into a fist. Took a breath. Looked at her. Took another breath and dialed it back. Wouldn't help anyone if he hit the guy. And if Annie loved the claim-jumper, Chris couldn't hit him. Not if Annie loved him.

He had only himself to blame. He'd put it off too long. He should have told her, right out, not just hinted. He had told her he was quitting, and they'd discussed it. But he hadn't said quitting forever. That he'd lost the wanderlust. He fingered the packet in his pocket. Hadn't said each time away from her got harder. He had said he planned to settle down. In Bear. Near her, he'd said. With her, he'd meant. Marry her. Hadn't said that.

"Boyfriend?" she asked. "No. Chris. No. He's a, um, a friend. There is no one else but you. There never has been. You know that. Please. Let's sit. I need to explain. I'm so nervous. Please." She tugged his arm and he gave in, mostly because it would put her announcement off a little longer. Give him more time to decide how to handle it. Maybe Chris *would* hit him.

She was jumpy. He'd never seen her like this; she'd always been cool and steady. And with the gang of kids she'd raised, there certainly had been opportunities to flip out. Did that mean she wasn't finding it so easy to break up? He hoped so. Anyhow, he would have a few more moments with her. Memorize her smile, her blue eyes, her shiny brown hair. Already burned into his heart.

She ordered sodas. Sodas? He didn't want soda. He wanted something stiff and hard but he'd settle for the soda with a twist. She couldn't seem to sit still, fidgeted. Stopped when a man stepped into the doorway. Her eyes followed the newcomer as he walked to the counter. She stared at him. Because she was nervous and couldn't look at Chris? Or because she knew this man too. Not tall, compact, solid. Brown hair. Chris couldn't see the color of his eyes. The guy looked competent. Was that why she watched him? The man sat and half turned. To watch the door? Them?

"Tell me again that you haven't found another man," he said. Please. Say it. She could fall for one guy, but two? No way.

"Oh, Chris, no. I could never love another man."

But she had brought him with her. And who was the other guy? He allowed himself to hope. "Okay. What's up? You're nervous as a penguin in the middle of a pod of killer whales. What is that man to you?"

"That man, um, ah, he's a ah a guy. A friend."

A friend. A *um, ah, friend*? Where had she met him? How long had she known him? Why was he here?

He felt the tissue packet in his pocket again. He'd had the rings made during this last tour by a friend who hammered gold jewelry. White gold, a matching pair. He waited for her to say more, but she didn't speak, just looked down at the table. Wringing her hands.

He sighed. "Start with the first guy. Not the one who just came in. You keep looking at him. Who is he?"

She turned and looked at the guy. "His name is Daffy. He's, um, he's watching me."

Chris started to stand, angry. "He's stalking you? That guy you're looking at? He's stalking you? I'll break his neck."

She grabbed his arm. "No. He is a friend. I told you. Daffy is protecting me. Not stalking. Guarding. Protecting."

That stopped him. "Guarding you? Why do you need a guard?"

"I'm in trouble. And one of my kids is too."

Not her biologic kids. But one of the Gang she fostered and protected. Her family. She raised the Gang while he traveled.

He sat back down. "What kind of trouble?"

"Bad trouble."

"Drugs?"

"No. Of course not." Aghast.

"You're sure? Because that other guy watching you is a cop."

She started to turn around, but he stopped her. "Don't look."

She closed her eyes a moment. "Oh. I know. Medium height? Medium build? White shirt like yours?"

She knew? She knew the guy was a cop? Was she in trouble with the police?

"Yeah."

"That's Ryan."

"Is Ryan for you or against you?"

"He's with Daffy. They're helping. He's not going to be happy you spotted him. Daffy's not going to be happy either."

"Well I didn't spot Daffy. You pointed him like a wolf eyeing a rabbit. And that made me extra sensitive to anything that didn't fit the background. Ryan doesn't fit. Tell me."

"He's married to Becca, you know, one of the Gang. Ryan is helping."

She'd told him about Ryan and Becca, Becca the cop.

"I am being stalked. Both Kevin and me."

Two guys guarding her. Two very competent looking guys. Chris didn't know what to say next. "Tell me."

"Wait." She looked straight at Daffy and motioned him over. Turned and did the same with Ryan.

"Daffy, Ryan, Chris," she introduced them. "He spotted you, Daffy. Both of you."

"Not surprised the way you kept looking at me. We'll have to work on that next time." Daffy smiled and rubbed her arm.

"You made me?" Ryan asked.

"Yes," Chris said. Nothing further.

Ryan sighed. "Okay. Let's all sit down. Annie, you tell him?"

She shook her head. "No. I haven't. Too much is going on in my head. You do it."

They all sat at the table sizing each other up. Apparently, everyone passed. For now.

"Short version," Ryan said. "Annie found a box of stolen jewelry. She told Kevin. Kevin contacted the sheriff who set up surveillance and caught the man who had hidden it."

"How did you know it was stolen?" Chris asked her.

"A description had been all over the news," Ryan answered for her. "We got the thief, or one of the thieves, but not the man who masterminded the theft. We believe that's a man by the name of Prowitt, a very nasty criminal. He's gone into seclusion. Kevin began to receive threatening phone calls from a no-name cell. From different no-name cells. This week he was attacked in town by four men. He fought them off."

"Fought off four men?"

"Yes. He is a black belt, and he was lucky. The same day, Annie was followed and threatened in town; next day her car tires were slashed. Two days ago, they made a grab for her, but Daffy was close by. Two of the goons got away, one is in the prison hospital, the fourth is in jail."

Chris swallowed hard. Looked at Annie. Took her hand. Turned back to Gibbs. "These crooks are after Annie and Kevin because they found the jewelry and turned it over to the cops?"

Ryan paused before replying. "That is what we think, because of the timing. Intimidation, revenge, payback. That jewelry represented a lot of money to Prowitt. And now, in addition to that, he has lost two men."

"If you know who he is, why is he still walking around?"

"Not enough proof to arrest him. Prowitt has multiple arrests, for burglary, assault, and assault with bodily harm. So far no convictions. In fact, none of the cases ever made it to trial. He always skates. He enjoys hurting people. Witnesses recant and disappear. We believe he has had them killed or killed them himself. I think the last."

Chris felt fear burn through him, fear for Annie. He stared at Ryan. Digesting both what was said and implied. Chris shook his head. This couldn't be real. "They've killed people?"

Ryan's lips tightened. "Never been proven."

Chris nodded once. Stood. He wanted to kick something, someone. He looked around the restaurant, at the people at the next table, a family eating and laughing. Normal.

"You knew she was in danger and you let her come here?" he asked quietly, outraged.

Ryan smiled. "We didn't *let* her come."

He found some restraint. Right. Annie did what she wanted. "Come on honey. We're going. We're catching the next plane out of here."

"And go where?" Ryan asked calmly.

"Anywhere. Doesn't matter. Away from here. I got money. Credit cards. Somewhere she'll be safe." He tugged her hand again but she wasn't budging. "Come on honey. We're getting out of here."

"I am not leaving. I am not running."

"What? Of course, you're leaving." He looked to Daffy, stupid name, for support.

Daffy shrugged his shoulders and his lips twitched before he spoke, "Might as well sit. We've been all through this with Annie. A number of times. She refuses to leave."

Chris leaned down, looked into her face. "This is your life we're talking about, sweetie. You're not safe here." He held her hand tightly.

She shook her head. "I'm not leaving my home. Prowitt is not running me out of my home. No one knows how long I'd have to be gone. Ryan and Daffy will keep me safe. They'll figure something out." She waved her free hand. "I'm staying. My life is here. I am not leaving."

He wanted to shake her, convince her to go, but he could see her mind was made up. He rubbed his hand over his mouth and chin. Ryan and Daffy exchanged a look.

Daffy said, "Ryan offered Annie a suite at his son's inn near Naples in Florida. She nixed it. My brother-in-law's fiancée offered a villa at his family's winery in France. She wasn't interested. She's not leaving."

The air went out of him and he sat. "You guys any good? Can you protect her?" he asked Ryan.

"Yeah. We can. We will. No one will hurt her. What about you? What are you going to do? If you stay in Bear, you'll be involved. The guy may decide you're a target." Ryan watched him closely.

"What happens if I don't stay in Bear?"

Annie gasped and he squeezed her hand.

"I'm just curious about the alternatives, honey," he told her.

"We continue to protect Annie."

"If I stay?"

"If you stay, you'll stay at the main house with Annie. It will be easier to protect you. We follow whenever either of you leave the property."

He nodded. "I'm staying. With Annie at the main house. As ordered." He grinned. Hey, it sounded like a win win. Ten minutes ago, he'd believed she was dumping him. Now he was going to be living with her.

"Guess I finally get to meet all your kids."

Annie snorted.

He turned to Ryan. Chris knew security when he saw it, he'd lived in some extremely remote and desolate locations on government research projects. Always with security.

Like any cop, Ryan had another question. "How did you make us?"

"Annie pointed out your friend here, otherwise I'd never have noticed him. After that I was looking at patterns. You didn't fit. Stationary when you should have been moving. You walk like the military police." He was putting them at ease with the step-by-step explanation. "What kind of a name is Daffy anyhow?"

Daffy shrugged but didn't reply.

Ryan stood. "Okay. I'll lead us back. You two in the middle and Daffy will bring up the rear."

"No. I don't think so," Chris said, not moving.

Ryan sat back down. "I thought you said you're going to stay in Bear."

"I am. But if you want me to follow orders, you're going to have to share information. Answer my questions."

Annie grinned, gave Ryan an I told-you-so look.

Ryan motioned to Daffy who said, "Daffy is short for Dieffenbachia, my last name. I'm married to Penney. She's one of Annie's, um, kids, as you call them, though I think Penney would prefer the term sister," he said with a half-smile.

"I'm a bodyguard by trade. Private bodyguard. Ryan here, last name Gibbs, just married another of Annie's, um, kids," he said with a quirky smile. "I like the term myself, but don't use it on Ryan's wife, Becca," he warned. "Gibbs is a cop. A fed. FBI."

It all clicked then. The names fell into place. The stories Annie had told. Penney had married Daffy, the bodyguard who had saved her life. And Gibbs had fallen for the cop. Chris studied him, could see him as an FBI agent. Nodded slowly.

Daffy continued. "Ryan's on vacation. Every time he takes a vacation, one of the gang gets jammed up and he has to work. We're not letting him take any more time off," Daffy said. "Becca knows your name and by now the whole gang knows. And they've had two hours to research you on the web, they know if you wear shorts of briefs."

Chris realized his mouth was open.

"Don't worry. They won't tell. They just always have to know everything."

Chris didn't care. "What are the cops doing to protect Annie?"

Daffy shook his head. "They're not involved officially. The threats are not overt, they're real subtle. The caller might say, *I'm worried about Annie driving by herself after dark.* Or *I think someone was following her in the grocery store.* That was the day after she mentioned some guy was watching her."

Gibbs took up the story. "We record the calls. The cops know about them, but they can't do anything since there have been no direct threats."

"The local cops are friends," Annie added. "They've been keeping an eye on me, too."

"Yeah. Unofficially. This family always needs help from the Sheriff," Ryan said.

"Because…?"

"Beats me. But seems like they have a way of finding trouble. Long stories which don't pertain to their current problem. Someone can fill you in later. Cav, the local sheriff, is very much involved unofficially." He paused. "It's not too late for you to back out."

"No way. Not if I'm sleeping with Annie." He winked at her when her color rose at his rephrasing of the situation.

Ryan watched him a minute and said, "Good. Let's get your luggage."

"I have a small duffle. Everything else was shipped. But first, if you two guys will leave, I want some time alone with my lady. This is not the way I planned our reunion." He waited until they stood and walked across the room, far enough not to be able to eavesdrop, but not out of sight.

"Did I make the wrong choice?" he asked Annie. "We can get on a plane to anywhere."

"I want to stay. I want you to stay with me."

"Good. I was worried you had gotten tired of waiting for me."

"No. I wasn't waiting, Chris. We were both doing what we wanted. You far away; me at home. You didn't leave me waiting any more than I made you wander. While you were off exploring remote wilderness areas of the world, I was helping a gang of neglected kids."

He pushed a strand of hair off her face, looked her in the eye, "I want to be with you."

"I want that too. We have to talk and make decisions, and we will, after you meet the kids and their friends."

"I just met two of the spouses and I'm impressed with anyone who raised a couple of girls who could attract men of that caliber." He leaned over and gave her a kiss. "I can't wait to meet the rest of them."

"I didn't really raise them. They raised themselves. Oh, I love you, Chris Nicolles." She threw her arms around him and kissed him hard. He returned it.

"We probably should hold this reunion later," he said and nodded in the direction of the two men. "Come on, let's get my duffle and find your car." And talk about our plans, he thought. My plans. For both of us. He put his arm around her shoulder and, neither of them paying any attention to Daffy or Ryan, walked to baggage. He grabbed his bag which was all alone on the stationary carousel, slung it over his shoulder with his coat and laptop, grasped her hand, and headed out into the parking lot.

He allowed himself one long glance across the tarmac to the helicopter hanger. Two choppers on the ground in front of it. He'd flown into Wilmington in New Castle, rather than into Philly or Dulles or any of the larger airports because he wanted to check out the facilities, spend some time looking around. He'd planned to look over the helicopters, take Annie with him. But he couldn't do that now. Later, he thought, and followed her through the small parking lot.

She stopped beside a dark green SUV and opened the back hatch. He threw his bags and jacket inside and walked her to the driver door. Instead of opening it, he leaned her back against it and stepped in close. He placed both hands on either side of her face and ran his thumbs gently across her lips. Gazed into her eyes as he leaned down and kissed her. A long slow passionate kiss filled with promise. When he finally broke it off, they were both breathing harder.

"There. That's the way I wanted to greet you. Tell you that I missed you. There is only you. When I'm with you, I feel whole. I can whip the world. When I left you this time, my world became gray and boring. I'm not leaving again. I'm staying, settling. You anchor me, brighten my world. This is our time now. Your kids are grown; my research is complete. I missed you so much, I wasn't sure I could complete this tour. I love you."

He'd never told her any of that before.

She gazed up at him with a slight smile, her tongue touching her upper lip. "I can feel how much you missed me. I love you too." She pressed her hips into him. "But Ryan and Daffy are watching and we have to get back. We're going to have to be patient because when we get to the house my kids will be there to check you out."

"I can wait. I've been waiting four months. I can wait a little longer. Let's go home." Home, he had said. Home. Bear. "And don't you worry about your kids; they're going to love me. Not just because they love you and you love me, but because I'm a nice guy. Besides. You raised them."

"Mostly they raised themselves, I made it possible for them to live together and be safe," she corrected him. "They'll give you a hard time."

"Stop worrying. I'm a loveable guy."

He leaned in for one more kiss. But stiffened when a threatening voice behind them sneered, "Well, isn't this a pretty sight. What's your boyfriend goin' to say when he finds out you're fucking another man?"

Chris spun around. Faced three men. Two of the men held guns. The third had brass knuckles on both hands. He was the one talking. "Maybe we all can have a little fun."

"I think you have us confused with someone else," Chris said with a calm he didn't feel.

"Not talking to you buddy. Talking to your whore. Guess she doesn't know old Kev has another little dolly. We'll get her next, after we give this one a message for old Kev." He flexed his fingers around the metal.

Chris shoved Annie behind him. "Get in the car," he told her. "Lock the door. Drive out of here." He took a step forward toward the thugs, away from the car to give her room. And he would need the space to maneuver.

"Tell us your message and leave," he ordered.

The guy's smile turned sadistic and held a gleam of excited anticipation as he rubbed the knuckles again. The set on his right hand had spikes. Those would really mess a person up. Chris hated to think what they would do to a face. Annie's face. The guy was dog meat.

"Oh, I'll be happy to give it to you. It's not a verbal message. More of a hands on. Right guys?" he nodded toward them and they laughed, enjoying the threat.

"She's going to be the message. I'm goin' to fix her face so no one ever looks at it again. Just a random mugging in the parking lot. But be happy to do you first. It will add to the message."

Chris risked a look for Ryan or Daffy. Saw no sign. Took another step toward the man. "Fine. What are you waiting for? All talk, no action?" Saw the anger in the guy's eyes. Angry people didn't fight well.

"Okay with me." The goon telegraphed his punch. Led with his right, the brass knuckles making him brave and stupid.

Chris sidestepped it. Caught the man's wrist with one hand, struck him in the side of the head with the edge of the other. Holding the thug by the arm, he twisted him around to use as a shield. The other two were standing open mouthed caught by surprise. Then one moved forward. The other raised his gun.

"Yoo-hoo. People. Yoo-hoo." A woman's breathy high-pitched voice called from behind the men.

Everyone froze. Then stared at the source. A woman. Not just any woman, but a beauty. Blonde, built. Long, long legs. Big hair. Waving at them. Bracelets dangling on her up-raised wrist. She moved in that awkward running motion women use when trying to walk fast in stilt heels and hers were impossibly high.

"Yoo-hoo," she repeated, red, red lips curved up in a sultry smile.

She didn't seem to notice the guns. Came closer. "Yoo-hoo," she called again. "My car won't start. Can someone help me?"

One of the thugs turned toward her and she effortlessly snatched the gun out of his hand, reversed it, and pressed the barrel up under his chin, she twisted his other arm up behind his back. The third punk stood with his mouth open. Again.

Ryan screeched to a stop and jumped out of his truck.

Daffy ran up. Both with weapons drawn. "FBI," Ryan said grabbing the third guy. He lowered him to the ground on his knees and cuffed him. Daffy came for the one Chris had immobilized. The woman suggested her guy get on his knees. When he didn't, she twisted his arm and forced him down.

The punk with the brass knuckles blustered, "Hey, these people attacked me and my buddies, we were just protecting ourselves."

Daffy cuffed him, removed the brass knuckles, and put them in his own pocket. "On the ground. Sit. Shut up," he told the creep.

Chris pulled Annie into his arms, held her close. She hadn't gotten into the car. He'd talk to her later about obeying orders.

Daffy secured the creep held by the woman while she kept her weapon on him.

Gibbs searched the three and collected more weapons and the woman handed her gun to Gibbs and said, "Well, that was fun." She turned to Annie. "This your guy? Becca said you were meeting your guy." Her voice was not seductively sultry now, but deeper, smooth like butter, and she didn't wait for an answer.

"Nice moves you got," she told Chris. "I might have been too late if you hadn't jumped in. I guess I should expect Annie to have a guy who is good on his feet." She didn't try for a handshake, instead moved in and gave him a hug. "You're family. I work with Daffy, for Jake. I'm Mary Lee or ML if you prefer."

Chris nodded.

"Gibbs had me sit on Annie's car, just in case. Smart guy," she said.

Ryan called airport security. Asked Daffy to call Cav to smooth their way with the locals. "He needs to know anyway."

"FBI ID won't do that?" Chris asked.

"Depends," Ryan said. "We'll try both."

Chris waited for the calls to be made, barley keeping his temper. "What took you so long to get here?"

Gibbs grunted. "I was at the gate and couldn't back up. Had to get on the highway to turn around. Screwed up. Thought you were right behind me."

The kiss. That had slowed Chris and Annie.

Gibbs continued, "My mistake. Daffy was at his truck. But Mary Lee was here." He nodded at the woman "You were safe. But it should not have happened." He didn't look happy with his mistake.

"Worked out," Chris conceded. "And you got these three guys." He looked at ML. She didn't look like much protection, but she had easily disarmed a guy almost twice her size, so he guessed she was good. And she had been here when they needed her.

Ryan scowled. "I underestimated Prowitt. I didn't expect his goons to resort to violence in so public a place. The lot is wide open, in full view of two highways."

"They didn't say Prowitt sent them, just that they were going to make Annie a message to Kevin, hurt her, disfigure her." Chris rubbed the back of his neck. "Wait. That guy," he pointed to the man who had worn the brass knuckles. "He said they were going after Annie's boyfriend's dolly next." Chris looked at Annie, was there still another man? "You have another boyfriend?"

She was shaking her head, puzzled. "No. Of course not. I don't know who he meant."

"Kevin. They think Kevin is your lover," Ryan said and asked, "Kevin has a girlfriend?"

She put her fingers to her lips.

"Does Kevin have a girlfriend?" Ryan repeated.

She nodded reluctantly. "He told me, in confidence."

Ryan grimaced, another mistake. Two in a row. But who would have thought Kevin of all people could have a private life? A life he didn't share? No excuse, it was still a screw up. Not too late to fix it though. "Who is she? Where does she live?"

"Tricia. I don't know where she's staying."

"Call him. I'll call Becca."

"Becca doesn't know. Kevin only told me because I guessed."

Ryan shook his head, "Never mind, I'll call him." He lifted his phone and hit a button, waited a moment. "Kevin. We're all okay, but Prowitt's men were here at the airport. One of them said they were going after your girlfriend next. Where does she live? I need your girl's address." He wrote in a small notebook he'd pulled from an inside pocket.

He listened a moment and said, "We're fine. Chris, Annie's guy, stopped them. And ML. I'm sending ML to Tricia and I'll have Jen and Ron head straight over. You call Tricia and tell her they're coming and not to answer the door until they get there and call you to identify them before she opens the door."

Chris could hear a loud voice from the phone, couldn't decipher words. Gibbs kept his voice calm. "No. Don't do anything. Wait for us to get back. Don't leave."

He listened, shaking his head. "We are spread too thin. Wait for us. Call her and tell her what's happening. Tell her to expect ML, Jen, and Ron." He paused, sighed. "Kevin, we need to keep everyone safe. Stay at the gatehouse. Okay?"

He nodded once sharply. "Good. Thanks. Let me talk to Becca." Gibbs turned his back on them and walked away, talking into the cell. He came back toward them, pushing buttons. "Ron, we need you. You and Jen." He explained the situation and repeated the address.

Chris, still holding Annie was impressed. The man could reach bodyguards with a simple phone call.

"Ron is Jake's partner. Jen is his wife. Jake is Cilla's husband. Daffy and ML work for them," Annie explained quickly. "It's a lot of names, but you'll get to meet them."

Two airport security cops came striding out of the terminal and Gibbs pocketed his phone and walked over to meet them. He pulled out his ID and explained the situation and pointed out the pile of weapons they had taken off the crooks.

The senior of the two men said, "We'll wait here for the sheriff; I called him. No sense moving everyone inside and then back out here. Tell me again what happened. Start with you." He pointed to Chris.

An hour later, Chris had repeated his story three more times. First to the airport cops, then to the detectives, and then again to the Cav person. The family sheriff. He was TV's idea of a small-town cop. Tall, good-looking, slow talking, definitely in charge. The uniformed officers gathered the prisoners and weapons, and everyone moved into the security office for the interrogation. They were finally allowed to go to their vehicles with a promise to sign statements.

Chris had seen Ryan look at his phone three times. Texts apparently. Daffy asked about them on the way to their vehicles.

"Kevin's girlfriend, the one he has been keeping to himself. Jen and Ron are with her. Becca convinced Kevin to wait for us. No telling how she did that. Hope she didn't hurt him."

"She wouldn't hurt him bad," Annie said. "How did they know I was here, Ryan? No one followed me."

"They stuck a GPS tracker on your car when they sliced your tires."

"Ryan Gibbs." She pointed an admonishing finger at him. "You knew that and didn't tell me? You know better than to keep secrets. How am I going to trust your decisions if you don't keep me informed?" He might not be one of her kids, but she treated him as one.

He wasn't cowed. "It was a judgement call, Annie. You didn't need the added worry. And Mary Lee was watching your car."

Annie stared at him in disbelief. "You were shielding me? Would you do that to Becca?" Because she knew he wouldn't. Becca would tear off his arm if she thought he was trying to shield her. She waited a beat and added. "Does Becca know about the GPS?"

Gibbs grimaced and Chris had a feeling the agent was caught between a rock and a hard place.

Annie put her hands on her hips. "She doesn't know, does she? Because she would have told me."

"She knows, but I swore her to secrecy. She wasn't happy about it, but I made a good case. So, you give her a break."

Mary Lee said, "Come on Annie. It wouldn't have made a difference except to upset you. We had you covered."

Annie eyed Mary Lee a moment and then frowned at Gibbs. "You and I are going to have a talk Ryan Gibbs. You will not keep secrets from me. And I'm going to have a stern talk with Becca."

Ryan said, "I made her promise, Annie. As a cop. She didn't like it, but she agreed. It's my fault. So, take your anger out on me."

Annie whipped around to Daffy. "What are you laughing at Daffy? You're in trouble too, and if Gibbs made Becca promise, how come Penney didn't tell me?"

Daffy choked. "Oh, no." He held up his hands, palms out and cheerfully blamed Gibbs. "It's all Ryan's fault. He wouldn't let me tell Penney. She can't keep a secret." He seemed to rethink the statement. "From her family," he added.

"We need to get out of here," Gibbs said, cutting the discussion short. "We can continue this argument back at the gatehouse."

Annie snorted and headed for the driver's door.

"I'm driving," Chris said, reaching for the keys.

She snatched her hand away. "I can drive." She tightened her grasp on the keys.

"Of course, you can," Chris agreed. And he knew she could, but she'd been through enough for one day and didn't need to prove anything to him. "I thought if I drove, you could tell me more about why men are stalking you. And, you know, you'll need both hands to do that." He waited.

"This one time," she said, accepting the honorable out and letting him know she understood what he was doing. He walked her around the car and helped her into the passenger seat, dropping a kiss on her hair. "Thank you," he whispered.

Ryan drove out first, Chris followed, Daffy next, leaving about three cars between them. Mary Lee headed for the Tricia person.

"How are you holding up?" Chris asked. His eyes flicked toward her and back to the road.

"Okay."

He waited for more.

She spoke slowly, feeling it out. "I don't know. I guess mostly I'm angry." She swung her arm. "Yes, angry."

He hadn't been expecting that. "Not worried? Scared? Anxious?

After what just happened? It's not too late to change your mind. We could leave town." He flicked a look in the rearview and turned back to her.

"No. I feel safe. Protected. The danger didn't seem real before those men showed up. I mean, I knew someone was out there and making threats, but it was just sort of an inconvenience at a bad time. The threat feels real now. But good people are watching me. They'll protect me. They are trained for this. I trust them. But they should trust me. They should have told me about the GPS thing. That makes me angry." She waved her arm and bumped the side window.

He glanced over and held her eyes for a few seconds and he went back to driving.

"You're trusting them with your life." He pointed out. "And they screwed up back there."

"Happens. And Ryan did have ML for backup. Yes, I trust them with my life. And I'm trusting them with yours too. But I can't let them think they can make decisions for me."

She had a point. She was an adult and deserved to know the full extent of the danger she was in. "I think I agree with that." And then he changed the subject. "Remind me how they all fit together. You never really shared a lot of details or, I see now, much information about their personal lives."

She'd taken the job ten years ago. He, going off to his first remote area research station; she, going to work for Kevin's parents as a nanny and housekeeper. Within a year, barely twenty-one herself, she'd been appointed property manager and guardian of fourteen-year-old Kevin. His parents were busy on a two-year around the world cruise. She'd discovered Kevin hiding four kids in the gatehouse. Computer nerds. She'd shepherded them all.

Annie smiled. "The Gang of Five." She took another minute, held up a hand and twisted it back and forth. "You know the basics. And some other stuff. But not their personal stuff. Not their business. Not their secrets. Not mine to tell. These are very private people who are extremely protective of each other. That includes me. They will protect me."

Yeah, he knew the basics. There were five kids to begin with. Kevin, John, Sarah, Penney, and Cilla. Cilla was the leader. She had organized them. Abused kids. And a couple like Kevin—kids ignored by their families—though Chris had always thought that parental indifference might be considered a form of abuse. He didn't know the details of their early lives. When Cilla found Kevin, she found a safe place for her friends—the gatehouse. Kevin's parents never went there. The kids hung out there. Lived there. Grew up there.

A couple of years later Cilla convinced The Boys, Joey and Danny, to move into the gatehouse. Chris smiled at that memory. Troublemakers, both of them, the same age, but enemies. They beat up on each other on a regular basis until Cilla got in the middle and showed them they could have a better life. Now they were brothers. One black, one white. Cilla added Becca a few months later. Becca was older and became a sort of house mother. Later, a sister. Tougher than either of them. Tougher than both of them put together, Annie had told him with a hoot. The three lived there together until Becca finished high school and college and joined the police force. Not Bear. Another city. She hadn't signed up with Cav.

John was engaged and in France with his fiancée. Sarah had married Michael and together they started a safe haven for abused kids.

He counted them off on his fingers again. Kevin, John, Sarah, Cilla. And Penney, the financial wizard. He realized he sort of knew Penney, married to Annie's bodyguard Daffy. He'd forgotten her story. Never connected it to his financial advisor.

There were no blood relations, but the Gang considered themselves family. Chris got that. He felt the same way about some people he'd worked with at remote outposts. You live and work with people, you come to depend on them.

"Well, tell me how they're capable enough to protect you so I can feel safe." He gave her a starting place. "Becca's a lot younger than Gibbs, isn't she?"

"She is. Fifteen years, I think. They don't see it as a problem. Newlyweds." She wrapped her hands together.

Chris was just a little jealous.

"He's helped the Gang with a couple of serious situations. I can't talk about some of that. Their secret to tell." She gave him a regretful half-smile. "An expression I'll probably use more. They each have a story. Becca married Ryan. I told you she was hurt on the job. I didn't tell you she was shot on duty and sidelined."

He gave her a quick glance. What was private about that? he wondered.

"She and Ryan found and arrested her shooter," said Annie, "and solved three other cold cases. His son Colin runs a security business, but in Florida."

She was silent a minute. "The Boys? Joey is ex-government something and Danny is a SEAL. We can call him if we need him. We have plenty of protection. Cav too. Which means access to all of Bear law enforcement. Take my word for it, the Gang has taken down a number of really bad people."

He nodded and checked his rear-view mirror. Daffy was still back there. He didn't see Mary Lee.

"Daffy?"

"Professional bodyguard. Mary Lee, also. Two of the best in the business. They work for Jake, Cilla's husband. He runs a business which has a need for people like them. That's all I can say about his work." She glanced over, and this time managed a smile, held up a finger. "That expression again. The Gang has used their services before."

They'd needed bodyguards before?

"Who are Ron and Jen?"

"Ron is part owner of Jake's business. Jen is, um, a sort of bodyguard and she is married to Ron. I've seen each of them go up against bad guys before. I trust them. I trust Ryan. He'll come up with a plan."

She looked over at him, pointed out the windshield. "Ryan will think he screwed up because those men got to us and threatened us. But Mary Lee was there. He'd planned her backup. She could have held them off herself. I've seen her in action too. Between the two of you I felt safe and protected. Ryan and Daffy were late but you took down the bad guys without any shots fired. Made it look easy. And now Cav has three thugs he can interrogate."

"Why didn't you get in the car and leave when I told you to run?" He tried to keep the anger out of his voice now, didn't think he succeeded.

"I almost did. But I wasn't going to leave you, three against one." Her turn to touch him, but it wasn't a comforting pat. She poked him. "I've been on my own a long time. I can take care of myself. I thought I could blow the car horn, but when I leaned in, I saw my emergency hammer."

"Your what?"

"You use it to break out a window if your car ends up in the water and sinks. It has a knife to cut a seatbelt. I decided two against three was better odds than one against three, especially if one of us was armed. But you grabbed that guy and slowed them down and then Mary Lee was there."

She hit him again. "I don't cut and run. If you don't like it, that's too bad. I wasn't made that way."

"I don't like it."

"I know you wanted me safe. Well, I wanted you safe. Let's agree to disagree."

He didn't like it. They'd talk about it again. He changed the subject. "Okay. Tell me how you found the jewelry.

She hugged herself and started in the middle. "Maybe you could say this whole thing is Arthur's fault. He laughed at Pauli."

"Who are Arthur and Pauli?" he asked bringing her back to the beginning maybe. He had a feeling this would be a long story.

"My girlfriend's children. Every couple of weeks we gather up the kids and visit her great aunt, Mrs. Hertog. She's lives alone. We bring fast food, tell tall tales, laugh. Mrs. Hertog has had a fascinating life." Annie turned in her seat and put a hand on his thigh. "Do you know, when she was five, her Daddy left them and went to live with another woman and her three children, children he fathered while married to her mother? Mrs. Hertog's mother. He deserted Mrs. Hertog and her mom. This was back, oh, long ago. Her mom had to board her out for three years. Worked all week. Visited every weekend."

Annie paused for a breath. Interesting story but he reminded her, "The jewelry, Annie."

"Oh. I'll tell you her story later. The kids always play in the granddaughter's room where there's a small table and four child size chairs and a tea set. Pauli makes tea for Arthur and the dolls. She doesn't really make tea. Just play tea."

Chris glanced at her.

"Of, course, you knew that. She's only five. Well, five and this many." Annie held up three fingers.

Chris bit the inside of his cheek and nodded. She'd tell it in her own way and at her own speed.

"We, us ladies, were in the kitchen when Pauli came in crying. 'Arthur laughed at me. I told him I was Wonder Woman, because I have her bracelet. See?' She was so cute; she had this gold cuff on her upper arm. 'It's too big for my wrist so I wear it up here.' And she took the cuff off to show us. She passed it to me and said, 'See Ms. Smallwood, it says Wonder Woman inside. I know it does because it has those two letters. The ones that look like two u's stuck together?' She showed me inside the cuff. 'See? You can read it. Tell Arthur it says Wonder Woman.'"

So maybe not the middle of the story.

"I looked at the inscription, holding it to the light. I expected it would say made in China. The inscription read, 'To my wonderful wife, Wonder Woman, Erine. Love you always, Richard'." She took a deep breath, placed her hand on her chest. "For a moment, my heart stopped."

Chris glanced over. "What was wrong with that?"

"Erine and Richard had been murdered in a home invasion a few days before. It was in all the newspapers."

"So, Pauli had the dead woman's bracelet?"

Annie nodded. "All the newspapers ran pictures of Erine and Richard at a big gala, a month before the killing and Erine was wearing that bracelet. The very bracelet I had in my hand. I scared Pauli when I asked where she got the bracelet. I didn't mean to, but she sensed my alarm and blubbered, 'I didn't steal it Ms. Smallwood. Honest. I didn't steal it. I just borrowed it.' She was only playing with it during the visit. Like she played with all the toys in that room.

"She was almost in tears. I patted her arm and told her it was okay. No one thought she stole it. We calmed her down. And Arthur gave her a cuddle. Mrs. Hertog had no idea where the cuff came from. Pauli said she found it in the closet in a box, and she took my hand and led us to the closet and pointed it out. A fancy box, one of those decorated ones like you buy for Christmas presents. The cover was off. It was full of jewelry."

Annie cupped her palms as if holding a package to demonstrate.

"Mrs. Hertog was shocked. She said her neighbor had asked her to keep the box for him; it was a surprise gift for his mom." Annie paused again, tilted her head. "I don't think I know why he couldn't keep the package in his own apartment, maybe his mother lived with him or would be visiting, and she might peek?"

Annie waved both her hands. "We gave the kids cookies and milk to go with their tea. Real cookies and milk. I took pictures of the bracelet and the inscription and emailed the pictures to Kevin with a text. He sent them to Cav. Sheriff Cavanaugh. He's a friend."

"I know who he is. I just met him. Remember?"

"Oh, right."

She was becoming tense again, and he didn't want that, she had calmed down when talking about the children. Now her movements were edgy. He wanted to wipe away the edgy. Hated it was there. Wanted to hunt down the man who put it there. And what? Throttle him? Didn't want to go there, so he asked about the boy. Annie's eyes had lit up when she'd mentioned the little boy who had tried to comfort his sister after he'd laughed at her and made her cry.

"Tell me more about the boy." He could fill in the gaps in the story later. And she talked about Arthur for the rest of the trip.

Chris followed Ryan when he made a right turn off the road and down a winding pebbled drive to an ornate iron gate where they waited for Daffy. Gibbs reached out and poked a keypad, Chris thought he spoke also. The metal gate rolled across the drive and the arm rose. They passed the small kiosk on the far side of the gate and drove down a hard-packed single lane road. He could see the roof of the main house above the trees. Took a left off the main drive around a curve to a quaint wooden one-story building. A carriage house. No, they called it a gatehouse. There was a bright garden in front of the wrap-around porch and flowering baskets hung from the eaves.

A man was pacing on the front porch and a slim, dark-haired woman stood in the doorway leaning against the jamb.

Ryan pulled in and parked and the man dashed off the porch and hurried to Ryan's window. Chris pulled in and parked beside Ryan. Daffy parked beside him.

The man declared, "I have to go to Tricia's, Gibbs. Now. I have to see for myself she's okay."

"She's okay, Kevin. I just talked to Jen; she and Ron are with her." Ryan exited his truck and motioned Kevin to the door. "Let's go inside. We need to make some decisions before you go anywhere."

"No, Gibbs. Now. I told Becca I'd wait for you to get back. But I'm going to Tricia."

Gibbs studied him a moment. Probably saw the same determination Chris saw. "Let me ask you a question first. How do these people know about Tricia?"

He shrugged. "I don't know. Why does how matter? They do know. She's in danger, and I'm going to her."

"It does matter. Think a minute before you go rushing off, putting her in more danger. Yourself too."

"How could I put her in more danger?"

"They might not know where she is, they may be trying to draw you out by threatening her. Then they will have both of you." He let Kevin think that over. "Let's go inside and talk."

The woman took Kevin's hand to lead him gently toward the door. "Come on Kev. You can wait a few more minutes and hear him out."

Kevin squared his jaw, his lips pressed together. He looked from one to the other. "Okay. Okay. Five minutes."

Chris and Annie followed them inside; Daffy brought up the rear. They stepped into a large open room. A sitting area in front of them, a large monitor hung over the fireplace and another monitor was on a side wall. A huge dining room table ran down the center of the room with chairs for twelve. A kitchen beyond that, separated from the rest of the room by a counter with stools for four. Chris could see two hallways, one on either side of the kitchen, reaching toward the back of the building. Computer work areas with desktops, laptops, and tablets were scattered around the perimeter. Posters for wall art. It resembled the communal rooms at outposts where Chris had worked, each station stamped by the individual's personal preferences.

Becca, he assumed this was the infamous Becca, told Gibbs,

"The jerk insists he's going to protect his girlfriend. I had to threaten to twist his ears to make him wait." Chris heard both love and concern in her voice.

Annie brought him over to Kevin, who stopped his pacing long enough to be introduced. "Kevin Esty, my boss. He owns the property. Christopher Nicolles."

Chris knew *boss* wasn't their exact relationship; Annie was housekeeper cum foster parent. "Mr. Gibbs says I'll be staying with you. I hope it's not an imposition," Chris said politely.

Manners took over and Kevin stopped pacing. "Annie will find you a room and take good care of you, I'm sure. You're welcome in my home as long as you care to stay." He gave Becca an angry look. "My sister Becca Gibbs."

"Pleased to meet you Becca." Chris walked over to her. "I like Ryan," he said with a smile. She examined him with cop eyes and gave Annie a small nod of approval before offering a hand. "Nice to meet you too, finally," she said with an emphasis on finally. "Sorry you find yourself mixed up in our situation."

"From what I've heard, doesn't sound like it's anyone's fault."

Daffy headed for the kitchen.

"Okay, Ryan," Kevin said, done with courtesy. "Talk."

Ryan sat at the table and motioned for Kevin to sit. He frowned but sat on the edge of a chair.

"Coffee? Anyone? Chris?" Daffy asked. He brought the pot to the table and went back for mugs.

Gibbs said, "They know about Tricia and we need to figure out how they know about her and if they know where she lives. If they do, we have to move her. The thug said they were going after *your other girlfriend* when they finished with Annie. Thug is in jail now, so he isn't going after anyone." Ryan raised his hand before Kevin could argue. "But Prowitt has other men he can send after Tricia. I doubt he can move this quickly, so for now, she is safe. Call her. Talk to her and calm yourself. Talk to Ron if you need to. We should get some answers before you rush off. We want her safe, Kevin." He spoke in a quiet, reasonable tone.

"That's what I've been telling him," Becca said a little angrily, "but he doesn't want to listen."

Kevin said, "I talked to Becca. And Jen. And Ron." He tapped the table with each name. "I want to be with her."

"We'll get the two of you together soon. Be patient a little while longer. Can you answer some questions?"

"Go ahead." He slid fully into the chair and reached for one of the mugs.

"Who knows about you and Tricia?"

Kevin's eyes went to Annie. "Annie."

Becca sighed. "Jerk's got a girlfriend and never even tells anyone. And not just any girlfriend, but my, um, aunt's daughter. Jeeze, he's seeing Tricia. And she's living in Cilla's condo. And no one tells me? I think I'll twist his ears on general principles. Keeping secrets like that."

Ryan coughed to cover a grin. Daffy snickered.

Becca turned her displeasure on Annie. "You knew. You knew and didn't tell me."

They stared at each other as Annie held her ground and Chris broke the uneasy silence speaking in a slow southern drawl, "Ah, ma'am? Are you going to hurt someone? Because I'm going to have to protect my woman here and I sure don't want my ears twisted."

Ryan laughed. "He's got a point Becca. Though that's the first time I've heard him speak with an accent."

Some of the tension eased as Becca transferred her angry scowl to Ryan. She sat and grabbed her own mug. Poured for herself and Kevin. Passed a filled mug to Annie.

Guess the fight was over, though, Chris noticed she didn't pour one for Ryan.

"No one else knows about you and Tricia?" Ryan asked Kevin again. "What about Cilla? It's her condo."

"Well, of course, Cilla knows Tricia's living in her condo," Kevin said sounding disgusted. "She doesn't know about me and Tricia. None of the Gang does. We weren't keeping it secret on purpose. It was still personal, never thought of sharing. It was," he shrugged, "just kind of nice to be by ourselves."

"So, the question still is how does Prowitt know?"

"Could they have put a tracker on Kevin's car like they did mine?" Annie asked.

"No. We checked," Ryan told her. Turned back to Kevin. "Could he have followed you, Kevin? Before Daffy came on?"

Kevin shrugged. "Maybe. I don't know. No. I haven't been there. We've both been too busy. Just phone calls, texting, Skype, Zoom."

"Any other way he could know about her? You haven't told anyone. Would she have?"

He shook his head. "No."

"I am going to guess you met her at the wedding."

"No. I already knew her."

Becca sat up at that. "How? You didn't mention it to me."

"Well, you were sort of busy getting married, Becca."

"I don't remember seeing you with her," Becca said thinking out loud. "Wait. I did. In the garden. You were talking to my, um, Aunt Nancy. She was there with you both."

Chris had lost track of people and relationships if he'd ever even known them. He seemed to remember Becca didn't have any relatives, let alone an, um, aunt.

Kevin told Becca, "We weren't involved then. Your aunt introduced Tricia and mentioned she was an attorney and we both realized we knew each other, had worked together before. By phone. That night we went out together and found we had some things in common." He bobbed his head back and forth with a small smile. "We liked each other. We clicked."

"So you clicked and she moved here to be near you?"

"No. Her move was already in the works. Bear is more central to her client base and she was already looking for a place. I told her to talk to Cilla about her condo."

Gibbs asked, "You said you worked with her before. In what capacity?"

"She's an attorney. Wills, estates, and trusts. I'm a Realtor, a real estate attorney, I broker real estate. Tricia's clients buy, sell, and hold real estate. I helped her clients." He stood. "How do I know how Prowitt found out about her? He's crazy." Kevin sounded defeated, confused.

Gibbs sighed. "How he found out about her and why he's going after her are important. Both for her protection and to help us arrest him."

"I. Don't. Know," Kevin said. "Can I go now?"

Gibbs nodded. "Think about it. Daffy will go with you. Okay, Daffy?"

"Sure. I'll bring him back too, right?"

"Yes. I want him here. We probably should move Tricia in also. Make it easier to protect her. What do you think, Kevin?"

At first, Kevin looked puzzled, his forehead wrinkled, then he eyes gleamed and he smiled. "Yes, I think she should move in with me to be safe."

"Here in the gatehouse," Becca teased.

"Main house," Kevin said, "but she'll take some convincing."

"You can do it, I'm sure," she replied dryly.

"I'll get a room ready," Annie said.

"She'll stay in my room."

Annie turned a light shade of pink. "Oh, well, of course. I'll freshen your linens."

"The linens are fine, Annie." Kevin patted her shoulder. "Stop fretting. I can take care of Tricia. If you need to fuss, fuss over Chris."

Chris smiled when Annie turned a darker pink.

Kevin gave her a kiss on the forehead, turning the pink to red. "Love you," he said and motioned to Daffy.

"Daffy," Gibbs said, "maybe go in and out the back way. They might have someone watching."

"Got it."

"I have a question," Chris said after they went out the door. "Why isn't this Prowitt guy after the man who managed to lose the jewelry? He's the one at fault. Shouldn't he be the first person Prowitt beats up? Even before he tracks down Kevin and Annie? Do we know who he is?"

"Yes. His name is Bob Evans. He has a long sheet, mostly burglary for hire, murder. And he is missing, so he may already be dead. If not, he's running for his life. Prowitt will kill him. That's his pattern."

Chris shook his head. "And the lady who owns the house where he stashed the jewelry? The kids? The kids' mother? Shouldn't you be guarding them?"

Becca answered thinking Annie's guy had a cop's talent for questions. "They are safe. Kevin sent them all to Florida on one of his jets. No record of their travel. They're staying with Ryan's son at a little inn south of Naples."

"So, he's after Annie and Kevin because he can't get to them? Because they turned the jewels over to the cops?"

"All good questions, none of which we have answers for. These three guys today may have answers. Cav will let us know."

"Well, Prowitt knows the cops have the jewelry, right? He's not after that?"

"In all the newspapers."

Chris shook his head. "That should make them safe, not put them in danger."

"You are right. Prowitt should not be after them. But he is. And until we get him, all of you stay on the grounds."

"No," Chris said. "I can't."

"What?" Becca said, standing.

"No. I can't," Chris repeated. "I have an interview tomorrow. For a job."

"Oh. A job." She glanced at Annie who raised a shoulder. "Can you postpone it?"

"Rather not. It's my future and I want to start on the right foot. I want this job. They want to hire me, but we both want a face-to-face first." He turned to Annie, "The helo job. We finalized the meet. Tomorrow." He turned back to Becca. "I have two more interviews later in the week. Those I can rearrange."

Becca nodded. "Okay. How are you planning to get to your interview? Borrow Annie's car?"

"I'd been planning on renting a car until I got settled. I still think I should."

"I agree. Because I don't want you driving a car with a GPS finder on it. Not that they won't follow you anyhow, but Daffy can run a long tail and Mary Lee will be backup. Where are you going?"

"Back to the airport. Little company called Helio Shuttle Service."

She didn't ask about the job, stuck to the basics. "If Prowitt checked at the airport, he knows who you are now. I'll make the arrangements to have a vehicle dropped off. About nine, so we can check it over. And speaking of tomorrow, Annie, Cilla is coming for supper. She wants to meet Mr. Nicolles and I imagine she'll have some things to say to Kevin."

Annie sighed. "Chris goes to his job interview and tomorrow evening he meets the Gang. It's going to be a busy day." She grabbed Chris's arm. "Lets head up to the house."

He was thankful when she waved the keys and headed for the door; he had just about decided that they would never be alone.

"They all know what we'll be doing in about ten minutes," he whispered as he stroked a hand down her back.

"Yes, they do, and I don't want to disappoint them." She drove the short distance to the main house where he grabbed her as soon as they stepped out of the car. He pulled her close to his front so she could feel his need, gave her a long kiss which she returned ardently. He pushed her away to look into her eyes and saw the same need.

"Don't want to disappoint your kids. We can come back for my bags." They walked into the house, never letting go of each other and barely made it to her bed where he pushed her gently down and she pulled him down on top of her.

Later they lay together. She on her back, a satisfied smile on her face. He on his side, watching her, running his hand slowly over her stomach. He loved the feel of her. Her skin so soft and warm. He loved her; always had. Never wanted anyone else. Never dallied with the lonely women at his posts. They didn't move him. Annie though, just thinking of Annie could make him hard.

The long separations weren't working for him any longer. He was ready for the whole package. Love, marriage, home, kids. He'd told her; the last time they'd been together, he was done with travel. With being alone. Could see the doubt in her eyes. Even long distance through Skype he could see it. But he'd give her time to understand he'd changed. He was pulling the plug. The wanderlust had wandered off to claim some other adventurer. He wanted roots. Stability. He hadn't been able to convince her long distance, but he would with her by his side.

She opened her eyes; stared into his face. The satisfied smile became wide and suggestive. "That was good. I needed fast and hard. Now I need long and slow."

This was the way it always was whenever they were together. Long sessions in bed. He couldn't get enough of her. Or she, him. They stopped talking for a very long time.

Lying with Annie's head on his shoulder and his fingers tapping out a random pattern on her arm, he said, "Marry me." He bit his lip, felt her stiffen. He hadn't meant to say that. It had just popped out.

"I'm sorry. I didn't intend to say that. At least, not now. I was going to wait until your friends had this guy in jail, but the words jumped out. Because that's what I want, I want you to marry me."

She leaned up on one arm and raised her head to search his face.

He took her hand. "I had it all planned, a romantic dinner, flowers, wine. Down on one knee, ring." He ran out of words and the ones that had come out were hoarse. "After a walk in the park, you have one; I googled it." He waited.

She was taking too long.

"Annie Smallwood, will you marry me?" he asked in desperation.

She pulled her legs under her, knelt on her knees. Didn't bother with covers. Gripped the hand holding hers. Kissed him softly.

"I love you. I have always loved you. I fell in love with you in grade school. You know that."

It wasn't a question, but he replied anyway. "I know. I fell in love with you then, too."

"We're different. You have wanderlust. You always have to see new, far away, remote places. I'm a stick-in-the-mud, stay-at-home with my feet in the dirt. What's going to happen in three weeks, a month, when you get that itch and need to leave?"

He started to tell her it wasn't going to happen, but she stopped him. "I'm sure that's the way you feel now, but you don't know how you'll feel in a month. I don't mind my lover being on the other side of the world for three or four months, but I want my husband at home by my side. My children's father here to raise them, watch them grow. I know it shouldn't make a difference, but for some reason it does. I can't explain it."

"I'm not going away again. I'm done. These last four months have been the worst of my life. I marked the days on my calendar until I could be back home with you."

"I'm afraid the bug will bite again."

He shook his head, managed a small smile. "I'm not going. I have a job lined up and maybe an investment in Bear planned. I want us to buy a house." He stopped, cajoled. "Say yes sweetheart. We can have a long engagement. A month. Two, you name it."

She studied him. "There's another problem."

"What?" he asked, wary.

"We don't know each other."

He knew her well enough to recognize the worry lines around her mouth and the narrowed eyes, so he didn't laugh at the absurdity. "What do you mean? We've been together forever." Maybe not together physically all that time, but together through the web. And whenever he was stateside and that was three or four times a year.

"Yes, but never for longer than a few weeks and it was always like a vacation. Play time. We made love, explored an exciting city, ate at new restaurants. We've never done humdrum, boring, ordinary everyday life. Wake up in the morning to fix breakfast and go to work. Come home at the end of a long day and do housework and cook dinner. Fix a leaking roof. Replace a broken washing machine. What we did wasn't real. We don't know each other. We don't know how we'll do living in the same house for an extended period of time."

She had a point. But, really, did anyone? "Okay. I'll agree, it wasn't real life. But that doesn't mean we don't know each other. Think about it. We decide together what to do, where to go."

She started to speak, but this time he stopped her. "Hear me out." He had to convince her. "I know you. We compromised on some things, renting a car, taking a cab or bus. How much to leave for a tip after a bad meal. Was it the kitchen's fault or the waiter's? You said the waiter shouldn't pay for the kitchen's fault. I know how you deal with people. I've seen you show kindness to salesclerks and strangers on the street and get angry at something on the news or social media. I know what you will do, what pushes your buttons, how you will react."

She didn't look convinced; he tried another angle. "Sure, we didn't have a leaky roof, how many couples do before they get married? But I know we'd discuss it, and get estimates, and repair or replace the roof. We'd buy a new washing machine, if we could afford it, a refurbished one if we couldn't."

She still looked doubtful; half convinced.

"I want to believe you're done wandering. I do believe that you think you are. Now. Today. But what about next month? Or three months from now when your feet start twitching? What happens then? I can't—won't—force you to stay. My husband will go and I'll be alone. Alone in a big empty house. Lonely. Waiting. I don't want that. This works for me, the way we do it now."

"We don't have to get married tomorrow. Say yes and we'll buy a house with Kevin's help and we'll move in together and wait for the roof to leak."

That brought a smile. He had her. The smile was always the first sign. And she thought they didn't know each other. "You don't even have to give me an answer now, think about it. When this Prowitt is behind bars, I'll ask again."

There was no one else for him. No one even tempted him. It had always been her. Her and some day. That day was now. He was ready to settle down. Her kids, as she called them, were grown. Now they'd find out if they could live together for more than two weeks at a time, in a town she already knew. They could. He knew they could. He wanted to wake up every morning with her beside him, share a newspaper over breakfast, fight over who got the editorial page first. And kids. He'd like a couple. They'd never discussed having their own kids.

He gave her a deep kiss and tumbled her over and under him. Subject closed.

They dressed slowly. "We better get your bags out of the car. Maybe scrounge something to eat, I have my own kitchen, or we can eat with Kevin, if he's back.

"Us, alone," he said. "We can meet with him later."

"I thought so, too. And I think he'll probably be occupied. Same as us."

She helped him unpack, then took him on a tour of the house. It was huge. "Kevin's parents built it. They were very much into ostentatious. Twenty-five rooms, eight baths, library, billiards, pool area with outdoor kitchen and bath. Originally, the house was a mess of towers, turrets, and roof gables. A lot of trims, all different with names I don't remember. Made me dizzy to look at it. Kevin redid the exterior and modified the roof, eliminating gables and towers. Left one turret. The house looks more sedate now. Instead of cold and formal, it's comfortable and livable. He knocked out walls, enlarging the living room, dining room, kitchen. Connected the three master bedrooms with sitting areas and bath for him. My wing was a sort of an off building attached to the main house. Now it blends into the structure. I have two bedrooms, a bath, sitting room, kitchen, dining area, office/sewing room. You've seen my bath." He had and admired it. Especially the indoor jacuzzi.

"The three-car garage used to be an eight-car garage and his parents were getting ready to add a barn for the overflow vehicles when they decided to go on that two-year cruise. Now the garage has extra bedrooms and bath. Sarah and her husband used it when they first started their home for lost children."

"What about the gatehouse?"

"That has two bedrooms and two baths. The kids use it."

"Not up here? The main house?"

"No. The gatehouse was their safehouse. Their refuge. It is where they grew up. Where their lives were forged. It's still Danny's home, when he's on leave and Ryan and Becca come for down time. It's where they all meet even now. Where they work. The computers are all cutting edge, bleeding edge. They keep them that way. Cilla is a program designer, John is too. The rest are all varying levels of geek."

They didn't hear from Kevin.

TUESDAY

Over a slow intimate breakfast Chris told Annie about his interview. "Not really an interview, but what else would I call it for your family? It's a formality to assure both Roger and me that we are compatible and can work together. If we are, I'm hired. We settled wage, hours, duties long ago in multiple emails and SKYPE."

Helio promised him a lot of variety, transporting people, equipment, and packages. Sightseeing tours. They even offered a package which let the customer make their own itinerary. He planned to expand that, add pilot training, maintenance.

"What about the teaching?" she asked

"Roger and I will talk some more today, but I'll be coordinating with the community college and the vocational technical school to offer flight training and helicopter maintenance at Helio. I can delay the in-person meet for the visiting professor position at the college. They like my proposed curriculum and I think we can safely say they'll be offering a course in the spring in remote area research."

"It's working out pretty smoothly," she said.

"We planned it well, you and me. Each step. Either way I'll be able to work at what excites me and teach what I love."

"Except nothing is normal right now. I'm sorry."

"Don't be sorry. None of this is your fault. Put the blame where it lies, on Prowitt. I wasn't going to start working right away anyhow. I told Roger I needed a couple of weeks down time. I better get moving. Don't want to be late for my first meeting.

Daffy drove the rental. Chris in the front passenger seat. ML in back. They waited with the car while Chris went inside.

The owner of Helio, Roger, met him at the door with a strong handshake. "Let's get some coffee and I'll show you around the area while we talk." Which was exactly what Chris wanted, a closer look at the facility and the birds, their maintenance. Roger talked a well-run shop and the FAA said good things about the company, but Chris wanted to see for himself before he committed. Another reason for the in-person meeting. Roger was curious about Chris's flying experience at his different duty stations, weather conditions, ground conditions, the birds he flew.

They talked as they walked through the main room and stepped into the hanger. The hanger floor was spotless shiny white. Roger pointed out neatly stacked and marked spare parts, boxed, shelved, and labeled on a balcony. Tools hung with-in easy reach on the walls.

"We buy new and military surplus. Dick, our mechanic checks everything as it comes in, enters it into inventory, and stores it. Each part has its own location. He and Pat, my wife, keep the inventory. Neither my wife nor I fly. Not because I don't want to," he tapped his chest, "permanent cardiac pacemaker. Fortunately got it late enough in life that it didn't hurt so much to stand down. Wife doesn't want to be a pilot. Doesn't mind co-pilot. We're both management."

They walked through the wide door and he pointed to the bird on the tarmac. "Go look her over, take your time."

A Bell 505 Jet Ranger X 5-seater. Chris's mouth watered. He loved the Bells. They did everything. He'd flown them to transport cargo and passengers, and twice, wounded and sick. He wanted one. He wanted a Bell. Someday when he grew up, he'd buy his own. Got to always want something, his dad used to say.

He took his time. The skin, tail and main rotors, hydraulics, fluid levels. He looked at everything the same as if this were a preflight inspection. The bird was well maintained and not just cleaned up for him today. It showed continual care.

Happy, he nodded as he walked back to Roger who was waiting patiently. "Good shape. Your mechanic does good work."

"Come back to the office. We have two more conditions to discuss," he said and led the way.

Conditions? What conditions? Chris had thought his employment was a done deal. No one had mentioned any conditions. He followed Roger into a meticulous office. The desk had three neatly organized piles of paperwork, no computer.

They sat, and Chris said, "You hadn't mentioned conditions before."

"Not conditions of employment. I decided to hire you a month ago, but I wanted to see you make that preflight inspection. The conditions, well they're sort of new. The County Sheriff hires us for aerial photography, maybe some marijuana searches, other stuff, and to assist in search and rescue. They can't pay a lot, enough to cover fuel, repair, and maintenance. Maybe a little left over for the pilot. We do it as a way of helping our community. You willing to volunteer your time?"

"That a condition for me getting the job?" Chris asked for clarification.

"No. No. It's voluntary."

"In that case, no problem. I want to be a member of this community and I'm happy to 'volunteer' flight time." At least he'd rack up flight hours.

"That's sort of what I hoped. You'll get whatever is left over after expenses."

Chris gave him a half smile. "What's the other condition? Something worse than flying for no pay?"

"The other condition is the Sheriff needs us right now. Elderly gent with dementia has wandered off, sometime overnight. The old guy got through the childproof locks on the doors. Sheriff has a ground search going but needs air help."

Roger pointed to the Bell. "All that bird needs is a pilot. She's ready. You just completed the preflight. Will you do it? Pat can ride with you, second pair of eyes and local information."

Chris laughed. Way to go. Fly? Now? "Sure." He stood, but then remembered. "I have to make a couple of calls first, I'm, ah, I have people waiting."

He pulled out his cell, which Kevin had tinkered with, so it was safe to use. Who should he call? The closest, Daffy? Or the boss. Who would that be? Gibbs? He settled on Daffy who picked up before the first ring ended.

"Daffy."

"I'm hired. My new boss wants me to go up and assist in a search and rescue. Now."

"You can do that? I mean just take a chopper up? No training? ID? Fingerprints?"

"Did all of that long distance and online. Everything but the face-to-face. I'm all set. I've flown this bird before." You never forget how to ride a bike. Or fly a Bell.

"Okay. How long?"

"Until we find him."

"Makes sense. Dumb question. Go ahead. You working for the Sheriff?"

"I think so. I didn't want to ask if that was Cavanaugh."

"It is. He'll keep us updated. I'll tell Ryan. Mary Lee and I'll be here when you get back. Good luck."

"Tell Annie?" Chris asked.

Daffy laughed. "Right after Ryan."

Pat had a clipboard and maps and showed him where the man had started and where the Sheriff wanted them to search. Next, she read off the man's description and the clothes he was wearing. Chris checked her flight plan; made one adjustment and they were off.

While he flew the grid, he asked Pat questions through the headphones.

"You never wanted to fly?"

"Never could. Bad eyes and reflexes. Safer for everyone if I just sit here. I don't get the charge out of it that you guys do." He gave her a quick glance, but she sounded okay with her status.

"How about Roger?"

"Oh yeah, he got the charge. He didn't like cabs or big trucks, and planes bored him. He flew for twenty years. But when his heart double-crossed him, he turned his energy to managementand running a successful transportation business. Picked the right time for that. This business was floundering. One chopper. No mechanic, no replacement parts. Place was a mess, waiting for him. The old guy who owned it liked Roger, took him on as manager, followed his advice. Left him the business when he died. A really nice man."

"How long have you been married?"

"Forever. Going on forty-seven years. We met in college."

"Always lived in Bear?"

"Moved here after we got married."

She knew what she was doing. Was a good lookout. They worked well together and were on their fifth transect when Chris spotted the gray shirt and radioed in the location. He hovered and circled overhead until the ground team arrived and signaled the man was okay. Then he headed back to the shop.

And home to Annie.

They were getting dressed after a shower together when the black-eyed daisy oil painting glowed and chimed.

"House phone," Annie said. She walked over and touched the flower and the image morphed into Kevin's face.

"Annie," he said with a sly smile. "I thought you and Chris should go with us to the gatehouse, together. You know, present a united front. What do you say?'

Annie lectured him. "I told you to tell them about Tricia, Kevin. You can't blame them if they're angry. But it's a good idea to go together. They'll go lighter on all of us. We'll be over in fifteen minutes."

"Thanks Annie," Kevin said with a sigh of relief and the image went back to the sunflower painting.

Chris was hopeful the gang would be more interested in Kevin and Tricia's romance than his and Annie's and that should help deflect his own interrogation.

"How does that work?" he asked pointing at the sunflower. "I thought it was a painting."

"It's a, well, like a giant tablet. Interactive."

"Can he watch us without us knowing?"

"Probably could; they're geeks. But they wouldn't."

Chris gave the screen a doubtful look, but he agreed with Annie. Kevin wouldn't spy. They finished dressing and entered the sunroom ten minutes later catching Tricia and Kevin in an embrace.

The woman—well she looked like a cute kid not an attorney— was medium height, well built, had dark layers of frizzy black hair. The glow on her face wasn't all embarrassment. She was dressed like Annie, only her crop jeans were pale green with a yellow T-shirt and matching yellow sandals. Why was he noticing shoes? Oh, purple nail polish on her toes. None on the fingernails.

She didn't look anything like Becca, but then they weren't even cousins, not blood relatives. Becca didn't have any. Did she? More non-related relatives.

Tricia took Annie's hand. "I'm so sorry Annie. I, we, never intended to put you in this position. I'll take full responsibility for keeping our relationship private." She followed that with a hug. And immediately turned to Chris. "I don't feel the least bit guilty

52

using your presence as a distraction and hoping it makes the Gang go easier on all of us." She paused a second. "It's nice to meet you."

Chris knew he should close his mouth and did manage to turn his lips into a wide smile. "I think I'm going to like you. I was planning to use you as a nice buffer for me. The way I see it, you're in for more trouble than Annie and I. Let's go face the music."

They drove to the gatehouse. Chris wasn't sure why; it wasn't a long walk. Maybe for a quick exit. A rusted out, dented, pickup truck was parked beside Ryan's truck.

"Oh, crap," Kevin grumbled.

"Second that," Annie groaned.

"What?" Tricia asked.

"Joey," they both said at the same time.

Kevin smiled weakly at Annie. "Hold my hand?"

She couldn't very well, she was holding Chris's in both of hers. She held them up to show him.

"Mentally," Kevin said. "We'll do that mentally. Show no weakness in the face of the enemy." He straightened his shoulders, patted Tricia's arm. "You don't have to worry, baby. It's me he'll flay."

"And when he gets done with Kevin, it will be my turn," Annie told her. "He's not going to be happy we left him out of the loop."

They walked inside with Kevin and Tricia in front.

Becca and Ryan were setting paper plates and bowls on the table. A younger, lanky guy was studying a computer monitor. "I found a list of his papers. Here's one, *A Treatise on the Effect of Below Zero Temperatures on Seismic Studies*. Sounds pretty dry."

"It's not actually. If you read it, you'll find they used some pretty weird methods to get results," Annie said.

Kevin told Chris. "That's Joey by the computer, Joey DePaulito. He's the short half of The Boys. The taller half is Danny. He's not here."

Joey, lean with long brown hair and the wisp of a beard, strode toward them all loose jointed. A bartender, Annie had said, for now, but soon an actor? He confronted Tricia, chiding her, "How could you go out with this guy? He's a nerd, a geek. And besides he's too old for you."

Kevin opened his mouth, but Tricia beat him to it. "You're right. He is a nerd, and he is a geek, but he's my geek. And he's the perfect age for me. I love my geek."

Kevin turned to her in surprise, but she ignored him and gave Joey a kiss on the cheek. "You're a good guy, Joey."

"I don't understand why you picked him over me. Or why you couldn't tell us." He punched Kevin on the shoulder, lightly. "And you, Kev. I thought we were best buds, we share everything, and you never said a word. I mean, I can understand leaving Becca out of the loop, but me?"

"What?" Becca howled in outrage.

Kevin raised his hands, palm out. "It was private. Personal. Just us."

"You told Annie," Becca accused.

"Right, you told Annie." Joey moved to Annie and put his hands on his hips. "Annie, you let me down."

"It wasn't any of your business, Joey DePaulito."

"It's not her fault," Kevin said. "When she guessed I was seeing someone, I asked her not to tell. And I didn't tell her it was Tricia."

Joey snorted. "She always knew more than we thought. She could keep a confidence, though." He moved over in front of Chris. "And here is one we've wondered about for years." He stuck out a hand. "Hi, I'm Joey."

Chris shook. "Chris."

"That's it? That's all the grief you're giving them?" Becca asked in feigned outrage. "I expected better from you. Danny will be disappointed."

"Danny's out of country or he'd be here, and I think he'd agree with me. Kevin and Tricia deserve to enjoy each other without our interference. And Annie? That's her job, listening to our secrets and keeping them. That's why we entrust our secrets with her, Becca, because we know she'll keep them and offer advice," Joey said.

"You are such a wuss." Becca shook her head, but more in pride than disappointment. And Chris gained more insight into how this *family* worked and how much Annie was a part of it.

Just then the security chimed and the large monitor came on. Chris looked up.

"Daffy and Penney," Becca said. "Cilla and Jake should be right behind them. They have pizza and salads."

Gripping his hand tighter, Annie warned Chris under her breath, "The family is arriving."

Penney, a tall striking redhead, walked in first. Walked directly over to Chris and Annie. "Daffy says you made him at the airport. Congratulations. No one has ever done that. I'm Penney." She hugged him. "You're Annie's special honey?"

He smiled. "Yes. Christopher Nicolles. Call me Chris."

She looked at him thoughtfully. "You can call me Penney or P. D. Wilkerson."

Huh. He shouldn't have been surprised. P. D. Wilkerson was his financial advisor.

Penney fixed Annie with a stern expression. "You never mentioned he was your special man."

Annie stared her right back. "You didn't need to know. You wouldn't have invested any differently if you had known."

That gave Penney only a moment's pause. "Of course not. But you could have told me he wasn't just a financial client."

"I wasn't ready to share that information when I sent him to you for financial advice. And it didn't seem important later. Forgive me?" she asked with a tentative tilt to her head.

Penney hugged her. "Yeah."

Chris realized he was witnessing more of the dynamics of this amazing family. Screw up, admit it, apologize, make up. "If it makes you feel any better, Penney, she didn't tell me you were one of her kids."

"We've taught her how to keep secrets well." Penney defended Annie, smiling and patting her on the arm. "It runs in the genes."

She gave Chris another hug, "I'd welcome you to the family, but Cilla is right behind us. She's the one you have to charm."

He was pretty sure he had won over the people in the room, but when he looked at Annie she was agreeing. "Cilla has final say." That comment really scared him. Cilla the matriarch of The Gang, the family. The two terms seemed to be interchangeable. Cilla was the one who had found them and rescued them. Brought them all together.

Shaking his head, he looked around the room again taking in the posters of Marissa, the star of a computer game. He grasped onto them as a safe change of subject.

"I never got into that game myself, but the guys at my last outpost said it's amazing. It's the only thing that kept them sane. They were always talking about Marissa." Everyone in the room stared at him and then at Annie.

Chris looked at her too. "What? Something else you didn't tell me. What? One of you is a high scorer?"

Annie touched his arm. "I told you they wrote a computer game; I didn't mention which game."

Chris knew his mouth was working but no words were coming out. Stunned, he sat.

Gibbs was laughing at him. "Go ahead say it. They've heard it before. They are effing rich. John wrote most of it and the rest of the Gang embellished it."

Chris found his voice. "I am really glad that I am sitting down. You all just go about your business; I'm going to stay here until my brain starts working again." Rich wasn't the right word. He knew the game had sold for hundreds of millions. Even split five ways, that was a lot of money. And there was a sequel in the works. And what about Joey? Or Danny or Becca? Did they help? Get a cut?

Penney took up the conversation. "Marissa, the game character, is based on Cilla's alter ego, Priscilla." He didn't get to hear about Cilla's alter ego as the woman in question walked in the door. Not the same woman as in the posters. This woman was small, sweet, casually dressed. The vamp in the posters wore four-inch heels, heavy makeup, a few important pieces of clothing. Marissa was the gaming version of this woman, hot and untouchable. A light went off in his head.

"Cilla, wife and mother." He pointed to a poster. "Marissa isn't an alter ego, she's the woman who created this family."

Cilla stopped short. Was she waiting? He took a chance. "Marissa might look like a vamp, but she's a savior. A man could live with her for a long, long time. I'm Chris, Cilla. I plan on living with Annie a long, long time."

Annie frowned.

Cilla smiled. "Okay then. You said all the right things. Give me a hug. Welcome to our family." And the rest of her family relaxed. "This is my husband, Jake Jayden," she said as a man came through the door carrying a small bundle. Not food. A baby.

"Joselyn," Cilla told Chris, as he moved forward to smile at the bundle. The baby reached up and grabbed a finger.

"Food's in the truck," Cilla announced, and Joey and Becca went for it. They came back with eight pizza boxes and two huge containers of salad. Must be more people coming, Chris thought.

"Please, sit, eat with us," Cilla said. "Ryan, Jake has more information on the guy following Annie the other day."

"Jake has info?" Chris must have asked that out loud because Cilla answered.

"Jake and Ron own a security firm. Their clients are mostly firms doing classified work for the government. They do background checks and provide personal security. You've met Daffy and Mary Lee, two of his employees."

"Yeah." Right, he knew some of that.

Penney set out glasses and silverware, Annie brought iced tea from the refrigerator. The security system announced another arrival, the sheriff. Cilla laughed. "Cav. I told him we had food."

"He'll want milk," Annie said reaching back in the fridge. Chris saw Cav look directly into the camera as he pushed buttons to open the gate. A good cop they said, and these people trusted him. "Why the Sheriff?" Chris asked. "I thought you said he wasn't involved with Annie's problem."

"The Sheriff is not only a friend of the family, but a member of our family," Cilla said.

"How does the Sheriff become a friend and a family member?"

"He's worked with us before on two or three cases."

"Us?"

Ryan explained, "The Gang. FBI. Becca's department. Us. Just accept that this family always needs a Sheriff, it seems they have a way of finding trouble. Cav is very much involved, unofficially, with the threats against Annie and Kevin."

Chris shrugged, felt a little more comfortable. Annie should be safe with both local law enforcement and the FBI helping. He glanced around the group and said to Annie, "I never realized there was so much you didn't tell me."

Cav walked in, took a quick glance around, and zeroed in on the baby and Jake. He walked over and took the baby.

Kevin opened pizza boxes and passed them around the table. "Vegetarian. Pineapple." He handed that one to Cilla. "You a vegan, Chris?"

"No. But I can eat it if you don't have pepperoni or anchovies."

Kevin made a face and Daffy groaned. "Does that mean I have to share my anchovies?"

"Thank goodness," Penney exclaimed. "I hate picking those little fish off my breakfast slice."

Daffy spoke around a mouthful. "She eats cold pizza for breakfast. Won't let me warm it up."

Ryan said, "Yeah, people are like that where she's from. How about you Chris? You from a place like that?"

Chris decided to ease into what they wanted to know. "Didn't know a taste for cold pizza was geographical. Whenever I get pizza, it's been hot, or I've been near a microwave. But I can get around a cold slice for breakfast." He paused and added, "I'm from Milwaukee."

Daffy took up the questioning. "Last time I was there, oh, maybe two years ago, got pizza at a hole in the wall called The Coffee Dock."

"Seriously, pizza at a coffee shop?" Chris asked.

"Yup. Pretty good actually, but no anchovies. Where should I have gone?"

"Don't know. Haven't been back in over ten years."

Pizzas and salad were passed around. Annie and Joey put dressings on the table, along with hot peppers and parmesan cheese. Cav was playing with the baby with one hand, the other already had a slice which was missing a bite.

"No family there?" Ryan asked.

They were getting to the real interrogation now and Chris was enjoying the subtle process. The gang was all personalities, and each knew how to quiz a person.

"Parents moved to Florida, place near Naples." He saw a look pass around the table. Over parents moving or the location? "Followed my sister."

Cilla asked, "Any other siblings?"

"Just Suzy."

Becca jumped in with, "Guess they like her better than you."

He jerked around to glare at her. Laughed. "Nah, it was the geography." They were good. He gave them a bit more. "Besides. I don't live anywhere."

That got Cav's attention, but it was Cilla who asked, "How can you not live anywhere? You must have an address." She looked to Joey who pulled out his iPad to search.

But Chris was used to this question and had developed a concise response. "I wanted to see the world. The remote, less traveled places. Some university or government agency is always doing research in those areas and needs people—scientists and support personnel. I select the remote area I want to visit and match my areas of expertise and specialties with what's needed at the site. Submit a resume or proposal. I just finished a four-month stint in the Antarctic recording a mixture of seismic studies and snow hydrology. That's the paper you found online, Joey."

Joey threw up his hands. "No address."

"What do you mean by seismic? How did you do that?" Gibbs asked. No address? He sent Cav a glance.

"Propagate sound waves."

"How?"

"Lots of different ways." Chris had a feeling Gibbs was looking for the word explosives, but he wasn't going to say it.

"Your specialty then would be geology? Hydrology? Seismology? Explosives?" Gibbs said.

"Whatever was needed."

"Ever carry a weapon?"

"Not a real one. The security personnel did."

"What do you mean, not a real one?"

"Well, some of the areas provided gun ranges, of a sort."

"Of a sort?"

"Yeah. Sort of a activity for downtime. Instead of solitaire or ping pong. Weapon hooked up to laser software for target practice. The equipment was intended for the security personnel, but we all used it. Kind of a kick. And no, I've never shot real bullets."

"I've used those," Becca said. "Cool."

"Where were you before that?" Penney asked.

"Reefs off Australia. Mapping corals and water temperatures and oxygen and carbon dioxide content."

"Wow. How long were you there?"

"Six months."

"Are corals geology?"

"Can be. I had a dual role there. I was part of support. I signed on as swing shift cook just to explore the area. Later I substituted for a scientist sent home sick."

"A cook?"

"Sure. Scientists need to eat. There are all sorts of support positions: mechanics, electricians, transport, data entry, pilots."

"What is the pay differential like?" Joey asked. "I mean between a scientist and a support person?"

"Not too bad. Probably made more as a cook. But money isn't the reason people apply."

Penney brought them back to research while she poured dressing on her salad. "What's it like? What do you do? How do you get a job in one of those places? What is your work schedule? Who keeps the timecards? How did you get started? How long have you been doing it?"

Her string of questions was met with laughter.

"That's Penney, never backward with her questions," Cilla said. "But I have to admit, I'm curious too." The rest were nodding.

"Started as a volunteer with the National Park Service while I was still in college. Worked during the off season. Yellowstone in the winter, Everglades in the summer. Then worked at Isle Royale National Park and Carlsbad Caverns, and Ft Jefferson National Monument. It was an easy step from there to the big time, the outposts. Park Service was sort of remote research lite. I've been at some outpost or other for the past 10 years."

Cilla passed him the salad dressing.

"As for timecards, no one keeps timecards. We are salaried. We were in an exciting location because we wanted to be, doing what we wanted to do. We often put in more than forty hours a week. On call twenty-four seven. There is a lot of work but a lot of down time, too. No restaurants, theaters, or nightclubs to help us through the long nights, longer weekends. You keep busy. Sleep, exercise, take classes. We share our knowledge or specialties with each other. Someone is always teaching something which someone else wants to learn. There is a wealth of experience. Sometimes the folks play video games." He nodded toward a poster.

"If the tour is long, they fly us home every three or four months. Did I answer all your questions, Penney?"

"So, what do you spend your money on?" Joey asked when Penney nodded.

"Nothing to spend it on where I'm stationed. I give most of it to Penney, she's been investing for me."

That statement got them. They all looked at Penney.

"Don't look at me. I didn't know he was Annie's honey until a few moments ago when we were introduced."

Chris said, "Annie didn't tell either of us. She recommended Penney as a financial guru and I sent her some money. It added up faster in her investments than in my own, so I sent her some more. Nowhere to spend it."

"Online," Joey said.

"Sure. But there's no way to get it delivered. No way to use whatever it is. So I saved."

"What are your plans now?" Gibbs asked. "Where are you going next?"

"Bear," he said, reached an arm over Annie's shoulder. "I'm moving to Bear. I'm done traveling. I want to settle, put down roots. Just having a hard time convincing Annie." He rubbed her shoulder.

"Planning on living with Annie in the big house?" Jake said casually.

"Planning on buying a place." He looked over at Kevin. "Can you be my realtor?"

"Buy? House or condo? How many rooms? Location? Downtown? By the water? Price range?" Kevin asked, easily side-tracked from the interrogation. Maybe he was Penney's blood relation after all. They both could ask a series of questions.

"I've done some looking online and have some ideas. Whatever we find, Annie has to like it. I'm pretty well set, thanks to Penney. Saved most of my salary. Like I said, few expenses and nowhere to spend the money locally. Besides it's hard to buy things if you have nowhere to store them."

A silence while they digested that along with the pizza. Before anyone could ask, he said, "I might have an offer to teach at the university; they're interested. I'd be a visiting professor. But I got a job this morning."

"A job? No one told me." Joey asked. "What kind?"

"Flying. That's my first love and Helio Shuttle Service hired me today. To fly helicopters."

"You fly choppers?" Joey asked grabbing the last slice in the pepperoni box.

"Yeah. I'm licensed to fly and instruct."

"When did you find time to learn how to fly? Where?" Penney asked.

"Remember I said there was a lot of down time? Whenever I had free time, I hung with the chopper pilots. They were friendly and happy to teach. We'd trade off with something I could teach. Sort of on-the-job-training. I learned a lot that way. I love choppers. There's a sense of real flight. The sheer pleasure of the wind beneath your wings. Or feet as the case may be."

He could teach flying or mechanics. He'd sent resumes to a dozen institutions and businesses specializing in remote area survival. He'd received no rejections; and a few requests for follow-up interviews. The university on the west coast had the best inducements, but he preferred a community college. He had a special place for them and their proud heritage in his heart. They offered programs with two-year degrees or certificates. Programs in exciting fields of nursing, fire rescue, computer science, flying.

Helio in New Castle wasn't even the best offer he had, but it was where he wanted to be because it was near Bear. He wouldn't ask Annie to move away from her family.

He'd start with flying, and if his financial advisor approved, he'd invest in Helio. That was a long-range goal.

Joey put down his pizza. "That's what I want to do. Fly a helicopter."

"Guess this is your chance to go out and do it," Becca said.

Annie nudged Chris as he stuffed pizza in his mouth.

Joey complained. "Yeah, yeah. Just always seems to be something else happening. It would be cool to include choppers in one of our games."

Annie nudged Chris again.

He scowled at her. "What?"

"Joey wants to learn to fly a helicopter," she said.

"Oh." He sighed. "If you're interested, I could take you up."

Joey's eyes lit up. "You would? Where?"

"Back at the airport. At Helio. I was going to take Annie over when I arrived, but things got complicated."

"Me too," Kevin said. "I want to learn. We might be able to barter a deal. My help finding a place, in exchange for flying lessons."

"We'll set some lessons up when things go back to normal."

"Wow," Joey said. "Wait 'til Danny finds out he didn't have to join the Navy to learn to fly."

Danny. Joey's brother. No, half-brother. Wait. Chris shook his head. None of the Gang was related by blood. Brother of the heart, that's what he was. Danny and Joey had lived together in the gatehouse while going to school. Becca had moved in with them. Annie was guardian and kept them on the straight and narrow.

"I have a new toy," Joey announced and picked up the padded envelope on the table and pulled out a stiff Styrofoam board. "Jif sent these. Her newest miniaturization." He passed the packet around. When it reached Chris, all he saw were buttons. He didn't have it long. Kevin pulled it out of his hands.

"Cameras. Miniature cameras?" He raised his eyes to Joey who looked very smug.

"Yup. Her specialty. Include audio. Transmit everything and record to the cloud."

Jif, one f, Chris remembered. She was earning her master's in physics and microelectronics; he was thankful her buttons had ended the inquisition. No one had asked about Annie and his intentions, only his background. There would be a round two.

"They're activated by a touch-and-hold. Try it."

Kevin pressed and held the red button and the monitors around the room came to life with Kevin's face peering out of them.

"Oh, wow. Does Danny know?" Kevin asked.

"I'm sure Jif tested them out on him."

"Let me see that." Becca snatched the tray from Kevin and her face replaced his. She pointed them toward Ryan and caught, for a second, a look of pure delight and love at her actions. She didn't see. She was looking at the button cameras. She turned them over to examine the back.

"They're earrings," she exclaimed.

"Two of them are studs," Joey acknowledged. "The red crystal is mine. The other four are magnetic and can be jewelry or buttons."

Becca turned the board over again and touched-and-held each button. Five views of her face, slightly offset, appeared on the monitors.

"Well, if the red stud is yours, that means the black onyx one is mine." Kevin grabbed them back and helped himself to one of the magnetic buttons which he stuck to his ear. Now one of the images showed the table. Two views of the table as Becca pinned a blue button to her shirt.

Three left.

Cilla reached for her own button and passed them to Penney, who fingered them gently and said, "Well, I don't know. Maybe we should save one for John and the last for Sarah."

Dessert brought the discussion around to the case.

Cav said, "Daffy, Ryan, can one of you explain to me exactly what happened at the airport? How did that go down?"

"I screwed up," Ryan said. "Twice."

"Oh yeah? How did you screw up?" Cav asked with interest.

"I underestimated Chris, got careless. He made me."

Cav turned to him, and said in amazement. "You? You made Gibbs?"

"Yeah," Chris said as if it were an everyday thing.

"Huh."

"Made me too," Daffy admitted. "The guy is not a simple researcher."

"No," Gibbs agreed, then added, "and then I was too far away when they needed me."

"Hmm. Guess it can happen. No one got hurt." Cav figured as long as folks were admitting mistakes, he'd pass along his short-comings. "Well then, I won't look so bad when I say we have no leads on Prowitt. The goons we arrested wouldn't talk without a lawyer and then they claimed they didn't know anything. Finally admitted some kook hired them in a bar. Never saw him before. Took his money. Half up front. Promised them more when the job was done. Job wasn't done; he probably won't show to pay up. But we'll be there."

"You believe them?" Ryan asked.

Cav nodded, sipped his milk. "Oh, yeah. They're lowlifes. Would have given Prowitt up for a free lunch. I worked those dirt bags most of the night hoping to get a line on him." He looked at Kevin with a question, but Kevin remained silent. Didn't volunteer any information.

Daffy put it out there. "I didn't say this, but someone probably hacked the FBI files." He didn't look at anyone. And both Ryan and Cav grimaced, because someone in this very room probably did and, though it was against the law and neither one of them approved, they'd let it pass.

Becca leaned back in her chair and smiled. "No one in this room would do that. Even if they could."

Cav frowned at her and she shrugged. But that only meant one of the other gang members had hacked the files. John probably. Cav had been hoping that one of the techno geek family members had found Prowitt. That they'd hacked a site which led to him.

"Can't blame anyone if they did some hacking," said Kevin. "They tried to hurt Annie. And besides, if we had done that, we didn't find anything. Nothing." His voice filled with disgust. "No chatter at all and we searched the dark net, too."

If they hadn't found Prowitt anywhere online, then no one could.

"Well he's older," Cav said. "Doesn't do the web. Probably as high tech as he gets is the multiple no-name flip phones he used to hire the thugs. And I'm even a little surprised he knew about burners." He put his milk down in disgust. Looked around for more cake. "No one else has heard from him or seen him. He's gone to ground."

He stood and stalked to the refrigerator. Gave it a glance, but decided he was too angry to eat.

Looked at Gibbs.

Ryan said, "I can't look officially, until I have cause. I don't like it either."

Cav knew. He'd arrested the creeps, hadn't he? And interrogated them. For all the good it had done. At least, Daffy was here. It was obvious the gang wasn't going to sit idly by and let anyone harm Annie. Or Kevin either. They'd tried for Kevin in town and he'd fought them off.

The Gang took his bad news well. Maybe because they hadn't had any more luck locating Prowitt than he'd had.

Ryan said, "I still don't understand how Prowitt can know about Tricia." He turned to her. "Tricia, think. Have you ever seen Prowitt? Met him?"

"No and no. I don't know him."

"He knows about you and Kevin. Have you told anyone? Maybe a girlfriend?"

Tricia shook her head.

"Your mother? Your brother. Someone at work? If we can figure out how he knows, it may help us find him."

"No. No. And no. I don't know that name and I didn't recognize his picture that Kevin showed me online. I don't know any of the people named as his associates."

"Oops," Kevin said.

She glanced at him. "Oh. I mean, if I had seen anyone online, I wouldn't recognize them."

Kevin smirked. "Good save, girl."

Everyone was quiet for a few minutes and Chris studied the people around the table. An interesting assortment, rather like one of his outposts. Penney, vibrant and outgoing. Cilla not pushy but still in charge. Jake quiet, but like Gibbs, and Daffy, it was superficial, covering strength and competence. Becca, another strong capable personality. Kevin appeared to be a little more fun, didn't take himself too seriously. But he'd taken down some thugs.

Annie said, "I've been thinking, wondering really. Two things."

Gibbs gave her his full attention. "What things Annie?"

"What I mean is, he gave Mrs. Hertog the box of jewelry and watched her hide it. Why?"

"So she doesn't peek inside?" Cav answered.

"When did that ever stop anyone from peeking? Didn't stop, Pauli. I can understand Mrs. Hertog not peeking. She's old fashioned. It would never occur to her. But Pauli looked in this box. Another question. Why doesn't he stick it in his own closet? Is it too full?"

Cav opened his mouth to explain and stopped. "Right. Why does he take it to Mrs. Hertog? We can ask him if we ever find him."

"And another thing," Annie ssid.

"That's three," Kevin said, and Annie gave him the eye.

"It's connected. Were there other boxes in the closet? If so, how many? And were they from other burglaries?"

"Christ. I didn't even think of that. But we searched. Would have found more if they were there," Cav said.

Gibbs tilted his head and gave Cav a look. "We missed that. Annie is thinking outside the box. Smart lady."

Chris had a question. "What about this Mrs. Hertog? Is she safe? Are you protecting her?"

"She took Ryan's offer of two weeks paid vacation in Naples at his son's Inn," Annie told him. "My friend and her children are not mentioned anywhere in the investigation, so they're safe. But they went too. Ryan's son is, um, ah, experienced in protection."

Cav said, "Might have to talk to her tonight."

"I'll call my son. Tell him you have questions for him to ask Mrs. Hertog."

Chris patted Annie's hand, as much to comfort her as himself.

Cilla picked out a piece of the cake. "Ryan. We need to get Annie clear of Prowitt."

"I may have an idea on that," Ryan said.

"Before you say anything, you should know we may have a slight hitch I haven't mentioned," Cav warned.

Two hours later, Cilla, Jake, Penney, and Daffy went home. Cav had been the first to leave, called out on an accident.

Twenty minutes later, Kevin shoved Chris out the door, jabbing him. Yelling. "Get out. Get out. Get off my property."

"What the hell? You can't kick me out," Chris screamed as he tried to grab the door jamb.

Kevin kicked him in the thigh and Chris went down to his knees, bent over, gripping the door. Kevin hit him with an uppercut and tumbled him out of the doorway and onto the porch.

"Get out. Get out," Kevin growled. They made eye contact and Kevin kicked him in the chest. Chris got both hands on Kevin's boot, slowing his fall, but he rolled down the stairs and hit the ground on his butt with a loud thump. He scooted backwards on his elbows, but Kevin charged him and kicked him in the side. "You get out." He emphasized that with another kick. "Leave." He kicked him again. "You're not welcome here."

Annie charged out screaming, "Stop. Stop. For God's sake stop, Kevin." She rushed around Kevin and dropped to the ground beside Chris, reaching for him. "Honey, are you okay? Let me see your poor face."

Kevin grabbed her arm and dragged her to her feet. "Get back in the house," he ordered.

"Kev—" she started to say.

"Do what I say," he screamed at her and backhanded her in the face. "I told you to stay away from him."

"Please. Please, don't hurt him," she wailed holding her face with both hands.

Kevin kicked Chris again and smiled as Chris curled into a ball protecting his middle. "Get up. I told you to stay away from my woman." And he shoved Annie toward the door where the others stood, immobile.

Becca ran down the stairs and gathered Annie into her arms. Cradling her, she walked her back to the deck.

Kevin kicked Chris one last time. "If I see you again, I'll shoot you."

He raised his hand and wiped his mouth smearing blood, turned to Gibbs. "Get him out of here. And I don't want to see you anymore either. Both of you. I see either of you again, I'm shooting."

"Becca?" Gibbs said, but she shook her head and walked inside.

Kevin followed her, taking the stairs two at a time. He slammed the door behind him so hard it flung open again.

The air in the gatehouse was thick with tension. Annie's hands were shaking as she stroked Becca's arms. "I don't believe it. I don't believe it," she said, her voice as shaky as her hands.

She took a breath. "I mean I don't believe that I believe it." She held out one shaking hand in front of them. "Look at me."

Becca grabbed it and held it. "It's okay Annie. It's okay. It's over." She spun around. "Quick, the window."

They crowded around the two front windows in time to see Chris roll over and try to kneel only to fall face first. He tried again and managed to stay on his knees.

Gibbs pulled him up by the arm and half dragged him, limping slowly to his truck. He sat Chris on the tailgate and rolled him into the bed. "Wish I had a cowboy hat to throw in after you," he said and slammed the tail gate. Leaned against it to get his breath. Pulled his keys from his pocket. Climbed stiffly into the truck, leaned back in his seat with his eyes closed for a few minutes then wiped his forehead and turned on the engine. Looked through the windshield and winked at them with a wild grin, backed jerkily, turned, and drove slowly out of the yard, hunched down low over the wheel, to dump Chris on a bench in front of the nearest motel.

"God, I don't believe it," Annie said again. "I knew it was a fake. I watched you practice it, but it looked so real." She had to stop for breath.

Joey grinned at her, all puffed up. "Well if they fooled you, they fooled those guys watching. It went good. Becca your ad lib gave it the perfect touch. Next time we'll plan a rescue into the choreography."

He nodded to the computer. "Our turn."

Kevin dashed over and hit three buttons. Loud angry voices

filled the room accompanied by sounds of breaking furniture, shattering glass. The noise boiled through the building and out the wide open door. It pounded through his head, but he was distracted when Joey squirted more ketchup under his nose and across his lips and down his chin. "Open your hand," he told Annie and filled it with the red condiment. "Remember to wipe it down your mouth and then wipe it off on your shirt."

"Becca, some for over your eye and on your shoulder. You need some cast-off." He squeezed some on her sleeve and down one leg. "Wipe," he whispered. Becca did, spreading the red down her neck and onto her shirt.

The yelling seemed to go on forever, but they had timed it at one minute forty-eight seconds. Timed it at a much lower decibel. First Joey yelling at Kevin. Then Joey at Annie. Becca at Kevin. Tricia. All five.

The noise ended abruptly, and the silence was just as painful.

Joey stomped angrily out the door and with one arm raised in a fist got in his truck and drove off.

"We're up," Kevin said and walked down the steps looking furiously toward the gate. Becca followed with an arm around a weeping Annie who had one hand holding her bloody cheek. Tricia brought up the rear; helped Becca catch Annie when she stumbled. They walked slowly to the main house.

Once inside, they collapsed in the living room. Annie and Tricia did. Becca and Kevin exchanged high fives and war whoops.

"I feel like I've been churned up by a tornado," Tricia said. "I guess I'm going to have to toughen up if I'm going to be living with that guy." She glanced over at Annie. "They look energized. How do they do that? How do you live with that?"

Annie snorted. "They've always been that way. Never back down. Will take on anyone. This was a new technique for them and, tomorrow I think I'll look back and smile. Right now, I'm going to try to stop shaking."

Kevin and Becca wound down about the time Annie got her breathing back to normal. "I'll put some coffee on and show you a room," she told Becca. "And we should all get this ketchup washed off."

"Hot chocolate for me," Becca said and put her arm over Annie's shoulder and walked with her to the kitchen. "And I'll make it. I hope your guy's okay. He sure acted hurt. I hurt and no one kicked me. Hot shower for my aches and pains."

"I feel sore too. But the whole thing was his idea. He's probably having a beer in the bar," Annie said. But she thought he would be doing the same. Sit, drink some water, take a hot shower.

Chris stayed stretched out on the bench a good fifteen minutes. Not because he was hurt, but because he just needed the quiet time. He didn't hurt but felt like he should. His own fault. He had suggested the charade after Cav announced a slight hitch. "There's a car parked in the turnoff. Two men watching the gatehouse." The table had gone silent.

"And you are telling us now?" Kevin asked a little belligerently.

"Had to let you finish your interrogation of Chris, here," Cav said. "And those guys aren't going anywhere."

Gibbs muttered, "Damn, I should have thought of that."

"You? Any one of us should have thought of it. We know people do that," Kevin said, pushing keys on his iPad. A split view of the overlook popped up on the monitors. A black Dodge with two men inside with binoculars. Side view and front view of the car. "I tried to buy that property after the last time people spied on us, but the state wasn't interested. I did install two cameras just in case."

"We might have a loud argument," Gibbs suggested. "I stomp out. They follow and tell Prowitt. Maybe he thinks I can help him gain access to you and Annie."

"Hmm," Joey said. "I got a better idea. Kevin and I have an

argument and take the fight outdoors. Exchange a few blows. Then I drive off. More believable. Besides no one is going to think an FBI agent will help them. A bartender? That's a different story."

"No fight. Argument and we both leave, separately. Give them two targets," Gibbs insisted.

"Argument won't work. Has to be a fight," Joey said.

Gibbs looked ready to start the argument, but Chris held up a finger. "Fight. And no one will believe you two fighting. Should be me and Kevin."

They stared at him. "Why would we fight?" Kevin asked.

"We could be fighting over Annie. Or Becca."

"Yes, a fight," Joey said standing and punching the air. "I'm taking this class in combat fighting and wrestling and working with stunt men, too, because I want to do my own stunts. I can teach you a few moves. We can practice, and then give them a show. And Chris can stomp off after it's all over."

Gibbs smiled. "That will work. No one gets hurt."

"Stage fighting only. I'll choreograph it," Joey said.

They'd practiced. Over and over. Joey made them practice the moves multiple times. Changed the scenario. Kevin was a natural. The boot in the chest took a few extra rehearsals. It had to be perfectly timed, so Chris could grab the boot to slow and direct his fall. Joey added Annie for more realism.

The gang had a hoot. That's all Chris could call it. He couldn't believe that he had volunteered to be the goat. His best buddy had always said, never volunteer. And he'd not only volunteered but insisted. Argued. Demanded. No one would believe Kevin and Joey would get in a brawl, but Kevin having a falling out with the new guy? The guy who was taking up with one, or two, of his women? It wasn't hard to convince them he was right. The watchers would fall for it. And then Chris had to prove he could act.

He shook his head and laughed at himself. At least he'd stopped shaking. Stumbled up from the bench Gibbs had 'dropped' him on and went inside to get a room. First floor. Easy access for anyone who wanted to talk to him.

He jumped when his cell sang.

They'd Skyped him. They were seated around the kitchen table. He saw a platter of cookies and Kevin pouring himself a shot of brandy. The others seemed to be drinking tea or coffee.

Chris rubbed a hand over his forehead. "You folks do this sort of thing often?"

"Only when we have to," Kevin replied.

"I can't believe you ran out there to help Annie, Becca." Chris shook his head.

"Joey almost ran out to rescue Annie," Kevin said. "She beat him to it."

Annie slapped him on the shoulder. "Rescue me? Since when do I need rescuing?"

"Since you were playing helpless, hysterical female?" Kevin asked.

"Oh. Right. I was, wasn't I," she said with a laugh. "That's kind of sweet of you guys." She sat back and savored the hot chocolate Becca had made for her.

Chris picked up the Coke he'd bought at the vending machine and was pleased his hand didn't shake, because his insides were still in turmoil. The Gang seemed calm. "You must lead an exciting life," he said. "How come Joey's taking, what did he call them, combat lessons? No one taught that at any of my remote sites."

"He's going to be an actor," Becca said with pride. "He's taking acting and dance lessons. He doesn't think I know about the dance; I'm going to spring that on him when he's not expecting it. But I didn't know about the stunt training. Seems like it might be a hard thing to learn, how to pull your punches. Don't think I'd ever need that."

Kevin snorted. "Right. You didn't practice fighting with Ryan at the trade show, or have that conversation with a ghost to con a suspect into a confession? You should be giving the class."

Becca tilted her head. "Hmm. It's an idea. All cops are born actors, today sure was fun."

It was Kevin's turn to punch her in the arm.

"Do you think those men might have followed me?" Chris asked. "Will approach me?"

"A good chance. They left right after you two. It would be logical."

"Wouldn't that be what they call entrapment?" he asked.

"How? We're practicing a fake fight scene. We're not responsible if they think it's real Those guys spied on us and decided to use you to get to Annie. Or me," Kevin said. "No entrapment there. Now, if Gibbs went to Prowitt with an offer, that would be entrapment. And we might try that, except we don't know which one of his places he's at."

"I'm not sure I'm comfortable with you out there all on your own," Annie said.

"He can take care of himself, and Mary Lee or Jen is close by," Becca told her. "Don't worry."

"What about Gibbs?" Chris asked. "Do you seriously believe a crook, like what you say Prowitt is, would contact an FBI agent? I mean, Prowitt would know he's a cop, right?"

"I'm not sure. He probably doesn't. But it's just the type of thing Prowitt might do. The unexpected. It would appeal to him to buy an agent. Wouldn't be surprised if he doesn't own one already. According to Cav, he always seems to know who the witnesses are and where to find them," Becca said. "We gave Prowitt a multiple-choice test. Choosing who to bribe gives him power. It will make him believe he's in control."

"You okay staying at the motel a day or two?" Kevin asked. Chris nodded.

"You don't have any more job interviews, do you?"

"None I can't postpone."

"What? I was kidding. I thought you got a job yesterday."

"Did, but I've lined up a couple of part time teaching positions. Interviews can wait. No one needs me to get back immediately, I'll postpone."

Becca changed the subject. "Look, be careful. You are their most logical choice. The new guy on the block. Watch yourself and wear your new camera."

"Will do."

She broke the connection.

WEDNESDAY

They were back in the kitchen for breakfast the next morning and talking with Chris on Skype again.

Kevin knew his way around a kitchen and was gilling sausage patties and bacon. Annie was scrambling eggs. Tricia was buttering toast. Becca set the table and poured drinks. No one suggested she cook.

"I've thought of a possible way Prowitt could know about Kevin and Tricia," Annie said.

"How?" Kevin asked. "I've been all over it. There's no way. We haven't been together since you found the jewelry." He stopped flipping bacon to raise his hands in a helpless motion. "He didn't tap my phone or lurk in our emails."

"How can you be so sure?" Tricia asked.

Kevin rolled his eyes. "I'm a geek and a hacker. We all are. No one eavesdrops on us. Give me a break."

"I was thinking," Annie said loudly, drowning his disgust. "Maybe he was a customer. Someone both you and Tricia worked with together. A buyer or a seller?"

"I don't know Annie. That's a lot of people," Tricia said. "I suppose I could make a list. Kevin could check it. But then what?"

Annie stirred eggs. "Maybe a name will match someone Cav arrested or is looking at. Or maybe another victim?"

"Wouldn't hurt to get a list together. Sales or purchases, her clients, my clients," Kevin agreed. "Give us something to do. Actually, it would be a pretty small list. Not more than fifteen or twenty names. We'll get started after breakfast. Joey texted he thinks he was approached last night. Some stranger asking questions. How long he worked at the bar? Know anyone who might be able to find him a condo? Joey said he gave short answers, nothing the guy couldn't find by asking a few patrons. Turns out he'd already done that, one of the waitresses told him."

"Guy asked about the bruise Joey had painted by his eye and Joey fed him a line of bull about how he'd got in a fight with this prick messing with his girl." Kevin laughed. "Joey's acting. He's having a great time. He learned bruises in his make-up class. Real loss to the intelligence community."

Chris chewed on that statement. Loss for the intelligence community? He'd ask Annie later. Meanwhile all this cooking was making him hungry.

Kevin said, "I did a search last night on the guy who left the jewelry with Mrs. Hertog, Annie. Nothing. That can happen, especially since I have little to go on. Not even a middle name."

"I can ask Cav for a middle name," Becca said.

"No. I looked at Cav's files. Used the initial and age. Twenty-six. Actually, I bracketed his age from twenty-two to thirty. No one is shown as living at his address or anywhere else that I could find. No work history, no medical records, not tax returns."

"You'd have found it if it were there?" Tricia asked.

"Oh, yeah." He looked at Annie. "I also ran Mrs. Hertog and your girlfriend, Annie."

"You looked at my friends?" she asked, shocked.

"Had to Annie. You know that. You'll like what I found. Your girlfriend volunteers with the USO and Meals on Wheels. Has a positive social media presence and sends letters and cookies to the men in her husband's unit. Your Mrs. Hertog? I want to meet that woman. Do you know she was the youngest person the railroad ever hired for the accounting department and the only one hired without a college degree? Hired her right out of high school. She still holds the record. And she worked her way up to V. P. long before she retired. I found a story about the railroad transferring her so she could follow her husband from duty station to duty station during the war while he served. Interesting person."

Annie beamed. "I knew some of that. She should write her memoirs." She transferred the eggs to a platter.

"I'm going out for breakfast," Chris said. "Watching you guys has made me realize I'm starving."

"Wear your camera," Becca said and clicked off.

"Tricia and I will get to work right after we clean up breakfast," Kevin said. "I'll go through all my files, separate out the sales I worked with Tricia, make a list of the people involved. Give it all a second look from today's perspective. Tricia, you should do the same thing working from your files. Then we can compare notes. Whoever this guy is, maybe he's in our files. Should be. But any of our clients could have said something to anyone." He raised his hand and twisted it palm up. "Who knows how many people? But we'll try. I can't meet with clients, so I'll start with my files when I finish phones calls and emails." He reached over and covered her hand with his. Annie thought more than files might be worked. Then he began gathering dirty dishes.

They were just finishing the cleanup when the kitchen cabinet morphed into a plate full of eggs, sunny side up, surrounded by sausage, potatoes, and toast. A dollop of ketchup fell on the egg yolks and a fork punched into them. Then the cabinet spoke. Chris said, "Get ready guys, we're on."

"What's he doing with those eggs? Ugh." Kevin asked.

A fork swirled the eggs and Chris said, "Didn't mean to drop the ketchup on the eggs. Guy just walked through the door. Oops, two more. I'll give you a look in a minute. These eggs sure put me in the moment, fit my character perfectly. Joey would be proud. Can he see? This is exactly what Dennis would do with his eggs, Joey. You told me to pick out a creep I know and emulate him. This is Dennis. But I don't know if I can follow through and actually eat these eggs." The fork scooped up some of the red and yellow syrupy eggs, moved toward the camera, to about where Chris's mouth would be, and went out of focus.

Annie seemed to realize she still had her cup in front of her mouth and took a swallow.

"I'm getting a location," Becca said. "Ally's Grill. Next door to Players where Joey works, so he's nearby if needed. Jif engineered a GPS tracker into the stud. Talk about miniaturization." She sat to watch Chris interact with the guy.

The fork went for a repeat motion and then the focus changed. Chris must have moved his head back, because now they saw a man's black suit jacket, red tie, white shirt, square broad shoulders moving toward the camera. Then the man sat, and they saw a neck and finally, a face. Square, with a flat, straight mouth, dark eyes under straight dark eyebrows. Hair, gray with streaks of white, cut short.

Back to the fork. Chris was tense, but excited. On a high. It was happening. He'd never really expected to be approached when he'd volunteered. But here he was, subtly morphed into Dennis. Dennis, sneaky, sly, stupid Dennis. And cocky.

"Hey, do I know you? Have a seat. Make yourself at home." Said it like Dennis would say it, with a frown and a layer of annoyance and sarcasm. He took a long look at the man's face for facial recognition. And scooped up some eggs with ketchup, Dennis would eat them this way. Picked up his coffee cup and raised it to the passing waitress and made a motion for a refill. Glanced around the room again, giving the Gang a look at the inside of the restaurant, the slight pause on the two thugs who had followed gray hair in wouldn't be noticed. Gibbs would notice the pause, but Gibbs wasn't here. He was out somewhere being bait. Chris was the one with a fish on the hook. His camera caught the two goons hovering by a table.

He gave gray hair a knowing smile. "Watcha want? Need something?" He said it with his mouth full, raised an eyebrow.

The man just stared at him, mean. Trying to intimidate him. Chris realized he was still hungry and grabbed the toast and shoved a corner in his mouth. Went for more egg. Chewing with his mouth open. Show him. The guy finally looked away and Chris swallowed.

When the man still didn't say anything, Chris tried again. "Or maybe you want something not so easy to get?" The waitress came by and refilled his coffee, set a cup in front of gray hair and poured.

"Give him the bill," Chris said.

The man finally spoke. "Want you to do me a favor. One I'm willing to pay for."

"How much?" That's what Dennis would ask first.

"Five hundred."

"I don't kill people." Finished chewing with his mouth open.

Disgusted, gray hair sighed, shook his head.

"Beat up someone? That will cost extra. You can have my ex for free." Suddenly, he wanted a smoke, which was strange, because he'd never smoked. But Dennis did, and Dennis would be getting nervous. He patted his empty pocket. "Got a smoke?"

"Don't smoke."

Chris went to work on his potatoes, smothering them with the ketchup. "Can't light up in here, anyhow. What do you want me to do for this theoretical five hundred?"

"Want you to call someone for me. Get them to come into town. Arrange a meet."

"Why don't you call him?

"He won't come to town for me. You're his buddy."

"Who?"

"Want you to call Kevin Esty and tell him to meet you here."

Chris snorted. "Nice talking to you." He leaned on the table to stand and the man motioned him to sit. Then laid out five one hundred-dollar bills.

Chris pursed his lips, stared at the cash, sat back down thoughtfully, and fingered the bruise on his face. From Kevin's boot. Carefully painted on last night and repaired this morning. Joey'd added a little gray green around the edges for a day aged. Maybe the same dye as Gray used on his sideburns. A bit too dark to be natural. He gentled his touch on the bruise and looked at the man.

"He doesn't like me right now," Chris said with a lopsided grin. "He won't come here."

"Make that seven-fifty for one phone call."

"I can make the call, but he won't come. You still pay me?"

The man was silent for a minute. "Take me out there, then. Just get me in the gate and the seven-fifty is yours."

"Can't do that, man." He patted his pocket again, because damn it, he really wanted that cigarette. He'd better pick up a spare pack and matches.

"Tell me the password. Seven-fifty is yours. I'll do it myself."

"Would like to, but you're a day too late. We had a sort of falling out yesterday." He fingered the bruise again. "But then I guess you know that."

"So, you got in a fight. You can still take me out there. You got the password."

"Kevin would have changed the password before I was off the property. Besides, the gate is voice activated." He eyed the money hungrily. Licked his lips. "Told you, call him. He's a businessman." Chris said the word as if it were synonymous with child molester. "Tell him you have a prime piece of property to sell or are looking to buy one. He'll meet you anywhere."

"Tried that. He didn't bite."

"No way I can get in there, man. Doesn't matter what you pay." Chris eyed the money again, stuck his tongue between his teeth, let a little fear in his eyes, glancing around anxiously. "I might be able to bring him out, but it will cost you a whole lot more that a measly seven-fifty."

Gray hair gave him a steely glare which didn't work on crafty Dennis.

"How much."

"Twenty grand."

"No way. Maybe, one grand."

Chris shrugged. "See ya."

"Fifteen hundred."

"Nope. Kevin's going to come after me. I'm going to have to get out of Dodge. Need seed money. You can think about it. You know where to find me. Half up front. Bring it with you."

He stood and was going to strut out, but the two thugs blocked his way. Shoved him back.

Gray didn't look up. "Sit. We're not done here."

Chris gulped, raised his hands palms out in a placating manner, and sat. "Okay. Okay. Take it easy, man. Take it easy." Licked his lips. "Just negotiating, man. You know." Tried a nervous laugh, channeling Dennis the night Chris had caught him selling drugs. Trying to sell drugs. Chris had turned him in. His eye twitched. "We can talk."

Gray hair stared. Silent. Threatening without saying a word.

How did he do that? Chris took note in case he ever needed to exude menace. Narrowed eyes. No lips showing. Heck. The man's ears were pink. Chris didn't think he could make his own ears turn pink. Maybe makeup? And why was he thinking like Joey? He wasn't an actor.

"Whatever you want, man. Whatever you want. I don't need to get beat up anymore." He touched the bruise.

The guy's ears got redder. "Shut up."

"Sure man. Sure." Chris backed up further into his seat smiling inside. Angry people were easy to manipulate.

Gray growled. "I'm not gonna touch you. But I may just let Bruno work you over with his little helper."

Little helper? Chris risked a glance. 'Bruno' was fingering brass knuckles on one hand. Brass knuckles with spikes. He gulped, and it wasn't acting. His hands shook. What was it about this town and brass knuckles?

"Bruno will show you what a real beat down is. Some torn flesh. Maybe scrape that bruise off your face. Fancy broken ribs? A broken kneecap?"

"Easy man. Easy. Never said I wouldn't do it. Either way, I get clobbered."

The menace turned to disgust. "Well, that's the nice part of this. You get to pick who puts you down. And anyway, Kevin won't be going after anyone. All you have to do is call the man. Get him here. You get the seven fifty and never see us again." He tapped the bills on the table.

Chris licked his lips; Dennis had done that. He pulled out his cell, laid it on the table. "He won't answer when he sees it's me calling."

Gray hair passed over his cell. "Use this."

Chris blinked. Really? The guy was going to give him his phone? He reached out hesitantly, held it in front of the camera, and pushed the contacts button. Only one number.

"He won't come. That's what I'm trying to tell you, man."

Gray nodded at Bruno.

"Wait, wait. I can't get him, but I can get his girl to come. Annie will come. And she can get him here." He tried a sly look made with slinky eyes. "Or she could get you inside."

Now the man sitting across from him smiled and Chris wished he hadn't. It sent shivers down his back.

"She'll come," he repeated and quickly added, "but you can't hurt her."

"Don't worry. We only want to talk to Esty. No one is going to get hurt. We talk to him, you get the nice money, and both you and Annie go on your way."

Right. Chris didn't believe him for a second. Everyone was going to get hurt.

Gray tapped the money again. "Get her here now, and I'll add another two fifty. An even grand."

Chris looked down and this time licked his lips over the money. "Okay. Um, my own phone." He was quick to explain. "I have a special ring. She'll answer for sure." The trembling in his hand as he dialed the phone was real. As it rang, he glanced nervously around the restaurant one more time. Everything looked normal, quiet, ordinary. A guy in overalls over there reading his paper, his hand searching the table for his coffee cup. A man in a suit jacket flirting with the waitress. Another examining the menu as if he'd never seen it before or as if it had changed this morning instead of a year ago. All normal routines.

The only anomaly was the two bruisers. One with brass knuckles.

And gray hair. "Put it on speaker," he ordered when Annie said, "Chris."

She'd watched the monitor and when her cell drummed Chris's ring, Kevin said, "You're on Annie. Ready?"

She firmed her lips, nodded. Took a breath. "I can do it."

She grabbed her phone. "Chris. Thank goodness. Are you okay? I was so afraid you wouldn't call. I just don't know what got into Kevin. I've never seen him so angry. Tell me you're okay." She whipped out the words breathlessly, the same way she'd practiced.

"Annie," Chris said hesitantly. "Annie."

"I'm here Chris. I'm here. Are you okay?"

"I'm okay, Annie. Few scrapes and bruises."

"You're sure? Because when he kicked you, I thought I heard something break."

"No. Nothing like that."

"Where are you?"

He half laughed. "Breakfast. Look, I really need to see you."

"Oh. I don't know Chris," she said with some hesitancy. "Kevin doesn't want you here. He deleted your codes, Chris, before you were even out the gate."

"You come to town. Meet me here in town."

"He won't like me meeting you."

"Don't tell him. Come on, Annie. I gotta see you." He tapped his toe, bounced his knee.

"I don't know, Chris. He was so angry. He hit Ryan, too," she added in a whisper.

"He hit Ryan? What happened?"

"They got in a fight and Ryan left."

"Becca go with him?"

"No." She shook her head to go with the word. Almost laughed at herself, because he couldn't see her, not with the cell phone he had. She got back to the script. "She reinjured her leg and is hobbling. Everything is such a mess." She let out a sob. "I'm so scared."

"Come see me Annie. Will you come or not Annie? Kevin doesn't own you," Chris added with a note of impatience.

Annie let the question hang there for a while. "Well, I want to see you. Touch you. Make sure you're okay. Okay. Yes. I'll think of some reason to go to town."

"Meet me at Players. It will be empty this time of day."

Another long pause.

"I don't think I should do that. If Kevin ever found out…" She let the statement drift off. Brushed her hair back with her hand. "I know. I'll tell him I'm going for a hair appointment. No. that won't work. He'd notice. Oh, I know a pedicure. I'll tell him I have an appointment. And there's a coffee shop right next door. We can meet there."

Gray's hand reached over and poked Chris. He mouthed *bar*.

"No. The bar."

"Wait, Becca wants to talk to you," Annie said.

"Annie," he called, but he was talking to air.

"Chris? This is Becca. I'm with Annie. Meet us at the coffee shop. Kevin will go ballistic if he finds out Annie met you at the bar."

Gray's eyes narrowed, and his forehead creased in anger. He shook his head furiously. "Annie only. At the bar," he growled.

Chris repeated it, growl and all.

"No, Chris. I'm coming with her. I need to see for myself you're okay. And it's better if we come together. Kevin won't question the two of us. We'll tell him we need cheering up. We could actually get a pedicure, after we meet, they do walk-ins. I want to see you. I need to see you. Please baby?" she pleaded. "Please. It's down the street from Players. Only half a block."

Gray was still shaking his head.

"Hold on a minute," Chris said and covered his phone.

"This will be better," he told Gray. "Becca will go along with whatever I ask, no questions. And Annie will follow her lead. You heard them. They're insistent. This will work. The coffee shop has booths. Like here."

Gray frowned, made the decision. "Coffee shop. Half hour."

"Okay, Becca. Coffee shop in half an hour. Can't wait to see you. And Annie," he added and disconnected.

Annie's hands shook. Becca was rubbing her shoulder, calming her. "Good job Annie. You pulled it off perfectly."

Annie put on a brave smile; sure everyone would recognize it for what it was. Now that it was done she couldn't sit still, anxious. "Let's do it," she said with more force than she meant. She didn't want to do it. But she couldn't sit and wait. And she had to do it before she lost her courage.

Kevin hugged her. "Go get 'em." He turned her camera on. "We'll be watching." He looked at Tricia to see if she might be panicking. She wasn't used to how the Gang worked. He'd been trying to protect her from the seemly side of some of the incidents the Gang had gotten into. Of, course she knew all about Becca and her story. But she was patting Annie encouragingly.

The two women gathered their purses and drove off, Annie with her stomach jumping nervously. Becca jumping in delight to be on an operation. Becca ran through possible scenarios. Came up with a 'safe' word. "Anytime I call you Ann, don't do anything or do the opposite of what I ask or say. Do whatever I tell you to do when I call you Annie. Simple."

Annie had to smile. She'd been expecting some code word, like pineapple, mango, or mercy. Instead she got a different version of her own name. She closed her eyes to reinforce the safe word.

"I can manage that. Never did respond to Ann." She bit her lower lip and her hands tightened on the steering wheel. They were going into an unknown danger, but Becca made it all sound normal, everyday. And it sort of was, for Becca. But Annie had always been on the sidelines of the Gang's adventures and was glad for the comfort of the safe word.

"So, you knew all along about Kevin and Tricia?" Becca asked, both changing the subject and giving her something else to think about. She didn't sound upset or outraged, just curious.

"Most of the time." Annie couldn't help her smile, the two were so happy together.

"Tell."

"Nothing to tell really. They were so sweet. So taken with each other. They were just so busy enjoying each other, hugging this happiness to themselves. Watching them? it warmed my heart that Kevin had finally found someone. She lights up his dark places. They weren't cutting you out. I doubt if it occurred to either of them to, you know, tell people."

"Yeah," Becca said, "she does make him happy. And he makes

her happy." She paused. "You and Chris too. You're like that. What's the story there?"

"You know most of it. Met in grammar school, been together ever since."

"Were you always in love?"

"I think I fell in love with him the first time I saw him, and I knew it the first time he pithed my frog in high school." She laughed remembering. "Yep, that was it."

"Why then? So he pithed your frog. Why do they do that in school anyway? Never mind. Tell me why then?"

"Because he didn't want to do it. He did his frog with his eyes closed, then he picked up mine. Ugh. I get the shudders just thinking about it. Anyhow he picked up my frog, frowned at it, glanced at me out of the corner of his eye. Pointed that thing at the frog, closed his eyes tight, and did it. Yuk. I fell for him completely. A guy would only do that for someone he loved."

Annie glanced over at Becca. "Kind of like you and Ryan. When he fell for you, it was written all over him. *This is the woman I love.* Kind of radiated off him." Annie laughed. "Everyone knew. Everyone but you. We were all wondering when you would catch on."

Becca's eyes opened wide in horror. "You were talking about me?"

"No. Becca. We were not talking about you. Well, maybe we were." It felt good to turn the tables on Becca. "Like you sometimes talk about me and my man. Only in the nicest and warmest manner. Don't act so outraged. Sarah told me she told you."

Becca settled back in her seat sulking. "Well yeah. She did tell me the Gang was talking. She didn't mention you."

"Don't get picky. We were all so happy for you. That cop face Ryan has? When he looked at you it was open for anyone to read. Just a matter of time until you realized you felt the same way. We had a lottery on how long it would take." She laughed out loud when Becca nearly jumped out of her seat.

"Again, only in the most loving way." Annie couldn't believe it. They were heading into a hazardous rendezvous which might end with kidnapping or injury—murder wasn't off the table—and Becca had her laughing at memories, laughing at Becca's outrage. Probably what Becca intended. The thought was sobering.

"We all know my story," Becca said changing the subject. "Tell about Chris. If you are so much in love, why is he mostly overseas and you here?"

Annie decided Becca deserved an answer. "He has wanderlust. Not just itchy feet, but a physical, emotional need to learn more about remote areas of the world, to experience them. He has to spend time in those places; live and work there. That's his life."

She shook her head. "I can't live like that. I need roots. I want to wake up in the same bed every day. I want a family. To be with my family. So, we agreed. We'd each live the way we want and we'd be together whenever he was between exotic places."

"Well I don't understand. Why not get married. People do that. Even I got married. You love him. He loves you. Obvious to all of us."

"When you talk about me?" Annie asked.

Becca didn't look embarrassed. "Right. And lots of married couples live apart. Look at all the military marriages."

"Won't work for me. I want to wake up in that room with my husband beside me. I want his face to be the first thing I see. I want to be able to touch him, hold him. For me, marriage means being together, not separated by oceans and continents."

"Does that mean you're looking for another man. One who can be a husband by your definition?"

"What? No. Chris is the only man for me. Always has been, always will be. I don't need a husband. Don't need the title of wife. Don't need a marriage certificate. I have him."

"What about now, though? He says he's staying. He just got that job."

"We'll wait and see. He has never before thought about settling down. We'll wait and see what happens."

"You'll give him a chance?"

"Of course, Becca. I love him. But the man has wanderlust in his blood. He may think he's ready to settle down now, but he might be lured off into the unknown next week or next month."

When she parked in front of the coffee shop, she realized Becca had totally distracted her. On purpose? Sure.

"Get out of the car Ann," she said, and Annie stopped herself with her hand halfway to the door handle.

"Good. Now, let's go and be brave while acting stupid," Becca instructed. But as Annie was opening the door it was slammed shut from the outside. She jerked back away from it and turned to look. A huge man had his hand on the door frame. One of the brutes in Chris's video. She froze.

"Don't move," he ordered in a gravelly voice. He didn't have to tell her. She couldn't move, even her breath was stuck in her throat.

But she did jerk when the passenger side door opened. She twisted her head a fraction, saw a hand reach in and grab Becca by the hair and drag her out, screaming. Dragged her to the back door. And then Gray filled Becca's spot. "He told you not to move."

Annie stared at him; her eyes wide. The man beside her door backed off.

"Hear me?" Gray said.

She managed a short nod.

Not the plan. Not the plan, she thought. This isn't our plan.

"Say it."

"I, I won't move," she whispered.

"Good." He nodded. "Now I want you to just relax. Chris is going to get in the back seat. With his girlfriend. And both my friends. That okay, Ann?" he asked politely. They didn't wait for her response. The man beside her pulled open the back door and pushed Chris inside.

"Ann?"

"Y-y-yes." The man was terrifying, exuding menace, and he didn't even have a gun.

Becca was wrenched around and tossed into the back seat to fall on Chris. The giant who had manhandled her sat beside them, the other brute took up position behind Annie, crowding Chris and Becca together into the center of the seat. Chris pulled Becca into his lap and she curled into him, mewling.

"Now," Gray said calmly, as if he did this every day. "Here's what you're going to do, Ann."

Her heart stopped when he called her Ann and she felt her eyes go wide. Her safe word. Then her brain took over. It was code only if Becca said it.

"Wha-what?" she asked. She wasn't faking the stammering. She was scared. Even more than she had been when the plan was hatched. "Who are you? What's happening? What do you want?" All those words came out in a rush.

"Shut up," he said. "First you're going to shut up."

Becca wailed, "Let me go. Let me go. Please let me go."

He turned toward Becca. "You, too. Shut up. I don't want to hear you."

Becca whimpered, and he raised his hand.

"Don't hurt me. Don't hurt me," Becca sobbed, cowering tighter into Chris's lap and he wrapped his arms around her cradling her protectively.

Gray smiled in satisfaction. Turned the smile on Annie, making her cringe back into the far corner of her seat.

"Good. Now, Ann. You are going to drive back home."

"Why?"

"I told you to shut up. You don't ask questions. You answer questions. You just do what you're told. You don't need to know why. Now what are you going to do, Ann? I want to hear you say it. Tell me what you are going to do."

"I, I'm, ah, going to drive home?"

"Good. Good." His smile was terrifying. She felt like a rabbit watching the fox.

"Now would be a good time Ann."

"Oh. Um. Yes." She made her shaking hand turn the ignition key and pulled out of her parking spot.

"That's my girl," he said.

Becca dared to ask in a high-pitched, whiny, little girl voice, "What do you want? Why are you doing this?"

Gray reached over the seat back and slapped her. She yelped and burrowed deeper into Chris who soothed her with a false confidence. "It's okay baby, it's okay. No one's going to get hurt."

"That's right," Gray said. "No one gets hurt. Be quiet. Don't ask questions. Do as you're told. We're just going to have a friendly visit with Mr. Esty."

"Why don't you call him," Annie asked without thinking.

He gave her the full wattage smile which had her cringing back again. "What did you tell me you were going to do Ann? Tell me again."

"Drive home." And she stared straight forward through the windshield gripping the wheel tightly. She was terrified. This wasn't the plan. What did Gray want? What was he going to do? Stop, she told herself. Stop. So what if this wasn't their plan. Kevin, Ryan, Cav, they'd protect her. Surely, they had a backup plan. Think of something else. Where were Ryan and Cav? Were they at the café?

Way back before the fake fight, Kevin had explained there were other ways to draw out the man threatening them, and Annie had made him enumerate them. Becca had listed three additional ways, but Annie could see their best choice was the plan which included her. They'd made plans. And backup plans.

"I can do it," she'd said. A fight and falling out over the women.

The men watching would contact Chris. He would call Annie and she would let the men into the compound. All she had to do in that version was open the gates. Then, when Gray changed the plan and wanted Annie to come to town, she'd agreed. "I can go meet Chris," she'd said with a lot more confidence then she'd felt, gripping her hands behind her back so no one could see them shaking. All she had to do was drive to town and meet Chris and Gray in the café. Get Gray to admit he'd murdered a man. Simple. No one had said how to get Gray to admit to murder. But Becca would know how to do that.

She'd been scared before, when she had taken responsibility for the gang. But it was a different kind of fear. It was a fear of failure. She'd jumped in whenever the kids needed her help. Stepped up. That first time when Cilla had been called to the principal's office for punching a boy, Annie had been all shaking nerves. Cilla was the one who calmed her. Annie had dressed formally, fixed her face, put on sensible shoes, and faced the principal. She'd spoken to him as if she were an attorney. She'd tricked the boy into admitting he'd harassed Cilla, slapped her first. Cilla said the kid was a bully and Annie presented evidence of it and then suggested the boy should be expelled. The principal had agreed. That had been her first success.

This fear, though, was visceral. Lives, literally, lives depended on her. Gray terrified her and Annie worried she would flake out. Jump out of the car. Run away. She wished she could be more like Becca. Becca was so brave, incredibly brave. Even as a child.

But Becca was whimpering in the back seat.

I can do this, Annie said to herself, just like I faced the principal.

She took two deep breaths. One step at a time. Ryan and Cav would rescue them. Her new role was simply to keep her family alive until they showed up. All she had to do was drive to the compound and open the gate. Ryan or Cav would be waiting. They wouldn't still be in the café. They'd have gone ahead. The thought calmed her. All she had to do was drive.

No one spoke, although there were occasional whimpers from the back seat, covered by Chris's soothing murmurs.

What did Gray want? Specifically. What did he want with Kevin? Why had he tried to kidnap Annie? Two times. To get to Kevin when capturing him directly had failed? Were they after Kevin because she had found the stolen jewelry and Kevin had turned it over to the police? It sort of made sense. But that didn't explain the threat against Tricia. How did Gray know about Tricia? She shook her head. These were the same questions Ryan and Cav were asking. Maybe once Gray confronted Kevin, they would learn the answers.

She dared a quick glance to the backseat and then through the back window. No cars back there. Where was Ryan? Cav? And what was wrong with Becca? She still had her head on Chris's shoulder. Becca was one of the bravest people Annie knew, so what was she doing still in that fetal position. Curled into a ball? Whimpering. She hadn't known Becca could whimper. Even when recovering from her gunshot wounds she hadn't whimpered, whined, or groaned. Suck in her breath? Yes. Mad? Again, yes. Moan? No. Not even when she was going through those weeks of therapy, which was as painful as the original injuries. But now Becca was holding Chris so tight you'd think her life depended on being stuck to him. Her fingers were curled into his arms the same way Annie's were tight around the steering wheel, knuckles white.

Holding him back? Was she making sure Chris didn't take on the crooks?

Annie tried to loosen her fingers. Concentrated. It wasn't easy. Her fingers were stiff and frozen. Chris's upper arms would be black and blue. The thought almost made her smile.

Becca was superwoman, not sissy girl. Annie wouldn't have been surprised if Becca had grabbed the two brutes and knocked their heads together. She almost giggled again. Yes, she was sure. Becca was holding Chris down so he wouldn't do anything foolish. The plan was to take down the boss. Plan A was to do it in the café, but they'd never gone inside.

Plan B must now be at the gatehouse. That's where Ryan would be waiting.

When Annie had agreed to the plan, she'd checked with Chris. Not sure why. She was her own person and could make her own decisions, but on some level, she must have wanted his approval. He'd simply smiled.

Gray broke into her thoughts. "Pay attention to the road and when we get to the gate, no funny business. Get us through the gate or your two friends in the backseat won't live very long." The evil menace in the threat was almost palpable.

Becca wailed, "Do it Annie. Push the button for Kevin so he will open the gate. And don't forget that x-code."

Annie almost said, "What?" Because they each had their own entrance code to open the gate. And the x-code shut down the inside monitors which allowed you to see who was at the gate from anywhere inside the house. It would announce three times it was implementing the x-code. The code also shut down the gate sensors and the keypad. Anyone wanting admittance just had to punch the large red button. Why did Becca want her to do that?

No one was at the gate. Maybe plan B was the house. Even with her hand shaking, Annie hit the right key. Pressed the x-code and smiled for the camera. The gates opened and a disembodied voice instructed her to come to the pool. She drove through. Saw the gates close behind her. Where was Ryan? Still behind them? Ryan would have to stop at the gate. Did he know to press the red button? Otherwise, the sensors would turn on the monitors and Gray would see him.

She drove to the front of the house and parked.

"You are going to sit there until I come around for you. And then you will take me to Kevin. Understand?"

She nodded.

"Say it."

"I'm going to s-sit here until, until, you come around and then I'll t-take you to Kevin."

"Very good."

Too afraid to look for Ryan or check the back seat, she watched him walk around the front of the car. Felt him open the door. He pulled her out and held her arm as they walked up the steps and into the house. She heard Chris and Becca, who was still weeping almost silently, walking behind them with the two brutes.

The Olympic pool had a rock waterfall and jacuzzi tub. Three separate conversation areas, a large dining table with seating for twelve, and an outdoor kitchen with a u-shaped counter with sink, stove, grill, small refrigerator and icemaker.

Kevin and Tricia were stretched out on an oversize boxy patio couch beside a circular table in the far corner in one of the conversation groups which included two matching chairs with tan cushions, all under a wooden shade structure, a sort of indoor/outdoor gazebo.

Chris hesitated when he stepped out into the open behind Annie and Gray. He'd expected to see the woods and trees beyond the pool. Instead he was in a tropical grotto. Kevin had lowered the painted privacy screens making the pool appear to be situated on a tropical sand beach surrounded by mountains. The thug behind him didn't notice the scenery and shoved him forward.

"Annie, you're back early," Kevin said, then stopped. Jumped up. "Why is he here? How dare you bring that man back here."

He bellowed at Chris, outraged, "How dare you come back here. Get out and take these, these, men whoever they are, with you."

"Calm down Mr. Esty. We'll be leaving soon enough. This is just a friendly visit."

"Out. Out of my house. I want you to leave."

"As soon as you hand over my boss's property," Gray said reasonably.

"Who's your boss? What property? How dare you come into my house!"

"My boss wants his key," Gray said.

"His key?"

"The one you took from his jewelry box stored at Mrs. Hertog's."

"What? You mean the stolen jewels? I never took anything from that box."

Gray shook his head. "Didn't think this would be easy. Just sit down and be quiet a minute please." He turned to one of the brutes, not the one with the brass knuckles. "Call Evens, have both of them come down. Go out front and meet them, bring them here. Mr. Esty will open the gate for them. Won't you Mr. Esty?"

"Who? Why would I do that? Get out of here."

"Because if you don't, my man here will use those brass knuckles on your pretty lady here. Her face." He stroked a finger gently down Annie's cheek. "Those spikes?" He shook his head. "You won't like what's left. Believe me. That type of damage? It never turns out well."

He shared a smile with the group and continued. "But if you will just turn over my boss's key and the address, my friends and I will leave, and you can forget we were ever here."

"You can't come barging in here and make ridiculous demands."

"Obviously, we can," Gray said in that same reasonable tone. "We're here. And we'll leave once I have the key."

"What key?" Kevin asked again, clearly puzzled. "Do you mean a house key? You want to look at a house? Which house? No problem. You could just call and say that. You don't have to bust in here." He became a realtor. "You must want to see the Sutherlands, multi-million-dollar estate. I'll get that key for you. You know the asking price, don't you? Seventeen point five million, but I know he'll come down. The place needs a little repair, hasn't been maintained and the landscaping is overgrown. You might want to redo it."

Kevin started to move around Gray.

"I'm not playing games here Mr. Esty and my patience has sadly run out. Don't make this any more difficult than it needs to be. You know I don't want a house key. Just hand over my boss's key and the wallet with the address."

Kevin said, obviously confused, "Um. What key? What wallet?"

"The one you took from the jewelry box." Gray smiled and Kevin took an immediate step back.

"I told you, I didn't take anything out of that box."

"Arnold told us he stashed it in that box, Mr. Esty. It's not listed on the police inventory. You had access to that box. You have the key."

Kevin shook his head, back and forth, but before he could deny it, Gray nodded to the larger ugly thug. The man slapped Kevin up the side of his head knocking him back three steps.

"Now see. I didn't want to do that," Gray said apologetically. "Just hand over the key or it's only going to get nastier. If you still play stupid, I'll have to call my boss. You don't want me to call him. Because he'll probably want to use the brass knuckles on your girl himself. Likes to do the messy stuff. Enjoys it. Give me the key and we're gone."

Chris didn't believe that. He didn't think anyone else in the room did either.

Gray continued in a reasonable tone. "It's easy. You turn the key over to me now and never meet my boss. Believe me, that would be your best choice. You will not like him."

The monitor pinged but didn't come on.

"That's my men. Let them in."

For a moment Kevin hesitated but then he pushed a button. He threw a nervous glance at Gray. "I don't know what you are talking about. I didn't take any key. The police have that box and everything in it."

"Kevy. Kevy. We both know that isn't true. The key was in the box. Arnold said that. After my boss asked him. He was under great distress at the time, because my boss believed he'd stolen it, filched it. Had sticky fingers and didn't think the boss would notice." Gray shook his head. "Can't tell you how unhappy that made my boss. No one steals from my boss. Especially not the thief he's hired to do a job. But my boss might have hurt Arnold a little more permanently than he intended. Or maybe just a little earlier than he intended." Gray frowned. "Seems the man had a, um, weak heart." He raised both hands in a helpless manner. "Who was to know? Now I don't want that to happen to you. Or to any of your nice friends here." He looked around the room.

"Who is this pretty girl?" He motioned to Tricia. "You got two? What about this one here?" He touched Annie's hair and she jerked her head away. He grabbed a handful and pulled her head back, arching her back. "That will be double the fun for my boss. Or triple with that one whimpering over there. He likes them to cry. Scream. He'll probably start with her. Or, I don't know. Save her for last."

"Stop!" Kevin yelled and moved forward, but one of the thugs hit him in the gut and he dropped to his knees gasping, clutching his stomach.

Chris started forward; Becca grabbed him in a strangle hold crying into his neck as the other thug moved in. "No Chris," she said and dug her fingers into the nerve when he tried to pull away. Surprised, he turned toward her. "No," she said and gave him a warning glare.

Gray raised an eyebrow at him. "You want to get in this, buddy? Which one's your girlfriend? Or do you share the women with Kevy here?" he asked and tossed Annie at him. Chris caught her and pulled her close. She buried her head in his neck on his other side when he tried to take a step toward Gray, she stumbled and fell taking him down onto the couch. Becca landed on top of him. "No," she breathed softly into his ear. "No. Stop. I'm okay."

He stroked her head, the spot where Gray had pulled her hair, took a deep breath. Took another deep breath. Where was Ryan? He wasn't sure he could keep up this act if Gray went after Annie again. He clamped his teeth together. Remembered he was Dennis of the cringe, the soft touch, the sly grin. Said sullenly, "She doesn't know anything."

Joey had told him to keep his mouth shut because tone of voice would be the hardest part to fake, but he felt he had the simpering, two-faced creep down pat.

"But she does, my friend. She was there. She saw Esty take it or she took it herself. I'm not a sexist. Could be either of them. Whichever it was, the other is complicit. I don't care if you think this is your woman or if you and Esty share both of them or all of them, but if my boss has to come here, we'll all get to share them." He nodded at the men who came into the room.

"Give me the key and we leave, Kevy."

"I don't have it. I told you. I didn't take anything from that box. Maybe he left the key in the house."

"You have it. Or the lady does. How about it Ann? You want to give me the key?"

She shook her head, her nose still in Chris's neck.

"Look at me," he ordered.

Chris let her turn to face Gray but kept his arms protectively around her.

"I need the key, the wallet. Or if not either of them, then the money."

"No. There wasn't any money." She shook her head. "No money, no wallet, no keys. Only jewelry. We don't have it. I never saw any wallet with or without money or a key. Only jewelry," she repeated.

"Okay. If that's the way you both want to play it, guess you get to meet the boss. Last chance. If I call him, people are going to be hurt. He enjoys hurting people. You don't want me to call him."

The group looked at him helplessly. "We can't tell you what we don't know. And these other people here are innocent," Kevin said, raised both hands helplessly.

Gray pulled out his cell, pushed one button, put the cell to his ear. "Yeah. We're in. They're not talking. Come in the front door. We're by the pool." He didn't say goodbye, just snapped his cell shut and sent one of the creeps out to wait by the door.

A flip phone? The guy was using a flip phone? How does a guy get to be a big criminal and still use a flip phone? Chris wondered, still holding Annie tight. Cav had said this Prowitt guy was technologically ignorant.

"Okay everyone, sit down. We wait. Boss likes to do the dirty work himself." He motioned to the thugs and they herded their captives to chairs around the table.

Chris hoped Ryan would come soon, though Ryan and Cav would be outnumbered.

"I told you," Kevin started to say and Gray frowned. "Sit. Shut up. This is the path you chose. Now choose to sit in that chair and be silent." He pointed. "Or you can be unconscious on the deck."

Tricia grabbed his arm and pulled him to a chair, and they sat silently to wait.

Chris glanced at Becca. She was leaning forward perched at the edge of her seat, looking down dejected, with one hand hanging down by her boot. She'd been amazing in the car. Whispering encouragement and instructions in his ear between fake wails and moans. There had been more than one performer in the car.

Fifteen minutes later the gate intercom beeped.

"Let them in," Gray instructed, and Kevin hesitated only for a moment before he opened the gate.

"Close it," Gray said. Kevin did.

Where was Ryan? Why wasn't he here? Or Daffy? Or Cav? Sure, the house was a change of location, but one they had discussed. Plan A, Annie lures Kevin into town, or Plan B have Annie bring the crooks back here. They had not discussed how the rescue team would get into the house now occupied by armed criminals. This wasn't quite the way they had planned it and Chris wanted to give Ryan and Cav and Becca credit for understanding their business, but he didn't see any good outcome.

How would Ryan get in? Would Gray let Kevin open the gate if Ryan beeped? Not unless Gray was expecting more men. Gray wouldn't see Gibbs on the monitor, it didn't seem to be working. It hadn't come on when the back-up bad guys entered. Did the crooks break it somehow? How could Gibbs effect a rescue with all these armed men pointing guns at them? Gray would shoot them if anyone came through the gate.

While Chris was trying to figure out the next step, a small rotund man walked in. He was accompanied by three more ugly brutes. Fatso sauntered over to Kevin. "Stand," he ordered. When Kevin hesitated, one of the men nudged him up with a gun barrel to the shoulder.

"I want to explain to you what will happen here. You give me what I want. We leave. You don't, we still leave, but you and your friends will not be alive when we do. You understand so far?"

"Yes. How do—" A thug slugged him, knocking him back.

"Shut up. and listen. I ask the questions. You answer them. Understand?"

Kevin nodded.

"Very simple. I want the key and address, the wallet, and the money which Arnold stole from me. His job was to bring me everything. He failed to do that. He died very painfully. A slow agonizing death. I made sure of that. Do you understand? Yes or no?"

"Yes."

"Now I want what's mine. Give it to me, I leave. I'll ask one time nicely. May I please have my property?"

Kevin shook his head. "We don't have it. Even if we did, how do we know you won't just kill us? We can identify you."

"But I'm not here. I'm with two senators in Washington. Now

before you say anything more, let me mention some people who did not give me what I wanted. The Rostoffs." He paused. Kevin blanched. "Ah, I see you recognize that name. I read in the paper that the family members were tortured and raped. Husband, wife, and children. I don't rape men, I let my employees do that. But the rest?" He spread his hands.

Prowitt let them see the pleasure he felt remembering. "I raped them myself. Not gently. While the husband watched. Made the sex even better." He nodded with a wicked self-satisfied smile.

"No children here. That's a little disappointing." He glanced around the room, looking each woman up and down. Annie shrank back into Chris's shoulder.

"Then there were the Andersons."

"That was murder suicide," Kevin said.

"My man here," he said, tipping his head to Gray, "set it up to look that way. Can't have too many families murdered. Authorities might start to get suspicious." He laughed evilly. "Same reason everyone burned, alive, at the Whites' residence. But not before suffering mutilations. Ah, I see you know those names too." He looked at Gray. "Here I think it will be murder suicide again. Over the women."

Gray nodded.

"No one will believe that," Kevin argued.

"Explain," Prowitt ordered Gray.

"People know there was a fight here. That this man was kicked a number of times and then dragged off the property and dropped on a bench in front of a motel. People at the motel will swear they heard him threaten to come back and kill everyone."

Kevin looked quickly at Chris. Wide eyed.

"No. No. I didn't. I didn't talk to anyone. I never…"

Prowitt frowned. "But this man heard you." He pointed to one of the thugs. "Didn't you Reginald."

"That's right. I heard him. He even said he was going to get what he wanted from the women first. Heard it myself. And there were other guys there too. Heard the same thing." He smiled. "And since I'm a good citizen, when I read about the murders, I'll go in and tell the cops. Just like I did when I heard about the Rostoffs. Tell my buddy cop here," he said motioning toward Gray who gave him a warning look.

"Shut up," Grey warned the thug at the same time Kevin said, "You're a cop?"

That explained the arrogance. And the crime scenes, Chris thought. Becca and Annie stared at Gray in dismay.

"See what you've done?" Gray said.

The thug complained, "What? None of these people will be repeating anything."

A thick silence filled the room.

"They might take Prowitt's deal. Of course, now that deal will include silence. Be smart folks. Otherwise there's going to be a lot of unhappy people here. Well some unhappy people."

"You- you're admitting that you killed those people?" Becca asked in a weak voice, shocked. "Tortured and raped them?"

"Well now, I didn't say that. He didn't either. But you can draw your own conclusions. You heard the boss here."

Becca faced Prowitt. Took a timid step toward him. "How could you?" she asked her arms spread and took another step.

"I did because I could," Prowitt said. "Just like I'm going to do here. Like I did the Whites. The only deal on the table is die easy or die hard. None of you will be alive tomorrow. We'll begin with you for daring to question me."

Becca stepped back, shook her head. "You're not going to touch me."

"And I suppose you're going to stop me? That's cute." Prowitt looked her up and down. "A little foreplay tussle will be good for both of us. I prefer blonds like Rostoff and her kids, but I can make an exception."

Becca snickered. Grinned. "That's all we need," she said and took one bold step forward. "Walter Prowitt," she declared, "you are under arrest for multiple counts of murder and grievous bodily harm."

He laughed and reached for her.

She grabbed his right wrist and pulled him toward her, spun him around in front of her as a shield and bent his arm high up behind his back.

Gray strode forward.

Prowitt bellowed, "You're dead. You're all dead. Get her."

Becca held her free hand up with her weapon pointing to the ceiling. "Stop."

They hesitated.

"Look around," she said.

While everyone's attention had been on Becca and Prowitt, Chris had pulled the small gun out of his back waistband and pushed Annie behind him.

Kevin had grabbed a weapon from under the chair arm and shoved Tricia down behind the bar.

"Don't anyone move. Please stand absolutely still. I don't want anyone to be shot by accident. I'm a cop," Becca said. "You are surrounded."

The privacy screens rolled up and the lagoon disappeared to be replaced by a phalanx of uniformed deputies in front of a row of marked squad cars.

Cav and Ryan came through the door. Deputies poured in behind them.

It was over.

The thugs were frisked and handcuffed. Their weapons confiscated. IDs were collected, some of which looked real.

When Chris was sure he could walk without shaking, he handed Becca her weapon back. "Why did you trust me with a gun. How did you know I could use it?"

"You told us you had practiced with the laser gun."

"Right." He was sorry he had doubted them. "Looks like you guys have done this type of thing before."

"Yup," she said with a smile. "Once, down at the gatehouse. A story for rainy day."

"You slipped him a gun? In the car?" Annie asked surprised.

"What did you think I was doing crawling all over him and whimpering?"

"I did wonder."

Prowitt was complaining non-stop. "You have no right. No right. Let us go. We have done nothing wrong. Just visiting our friend here."

"Shut up," Cav told him and read him his rights.

"I demand my attorney. I'll have your job."

"You should stop talking. You can call your attorney from the station."

"I have done nothing. I don't know who these men are. I never saw them before. They pushed their way in behind me. They must work for that Esty guy. They are his thugs. He brought them here to intimidate me," he blustered. "I only came to get my key. This man stole my key. Search him. You'll find it."

"We can do that. You're saying he stole your key."

"Yes. He stole my key and my wallet. He stole those. He's probably already spent my gold coins. They're probably gone." Prowitt said the last with a crafty bluster which screamed a lie.

"What type of key are we looking for? House key? Safe deposit key?" Cav asked.

"Like a key, idiot. I'm not going to describe it. He won't be able to tell you what it's for. Ask him. It's in the wallet. The wallet he stole."

"What does the wallet look like?"

Prowitt shook his head. "I'm not saying any more. Ask him. Make him show you."

"Mr. Esty?"

"I don't know what he is talking about. I don't have anything that belongs to him."

Prowitt couldn't contain himself. "The key. It opens my vault."

"What about the address you want?" Cav asked.

"It's the address of the vault. He won't know that address and I'm not revealing it. Not giving him a chance to go steal the rest of my gold." He smiled as if he had made a point.

Cav nodded.

"Search this place. You'll find my things. He has them. He was holding them for ransom. Demanded that I come here today. Now I want my attorney. This is all a horrible mistake."

Cav smiled at him. "It's all on tape, Prowitt. Every word you said since you entered the gate. I advise you again to be quiet."

"That's not legal. You can't use a secret recording. It will never stand up in court. You can't tape people without permission and I never gave it."

Cav shook his head. "Signs out there at the entrance gate. Premises under video surveillance. It will hold up all right."

Prowitt shrugged, changed his story. "Doesn't matter. I was kidding. Just joking. Didn't mean a word of anything I said. I was trying to scare him."

"The video is enough for a search warrant for your properties. Request has already gone out to a judge. All your homes. Bank vaults. Vehicles. What do you want to bet we find property belonging to the Rostoffs, Andersons, and Whites?"

Prowitt blanched with his lips pressed tight together. "My lawyer will have your job if you do that."

"Get these men out of here," Cav said and grabbed Prowitt to lead him out.

Chris sat down hard. Pulled Annie with him. "Wow," he said. "Wow. I thought we were dead."

Kevin fetched coffee and tea from the kitchen. Tricia helped.

Chris took a deep breath. "How did you do that, Ryan? How did you get in? The gate was locked. How did you get all those vehicles in. When?" He stopped. Took a breath. Maybe he'd caught the gift of many questions from Penney. He smiled. That would make him a member of the family. Have to mention it to Annie later.

Ryan laughed. Pointed at Becca. "Her idea."

"Sorry Chris, you were gone when we set it up. Annie, that's why I had you use the special code. Kevin programmed it to disable everything except the one button for entry. Ryan, Cav, all of them could get in without the main building being notified and that's exactly what they did."

Ryan took up the tale. "We used the ridge lookout for a staging area as soon as the two goons left. When the gray-haired guy—"

"Gray, I think of him as Gray," Becca interrupted.

"Me too," Annie said.

"A cop. You heard," Becca added.

"As soon as 'Gray' called his men off the ridge, we set up and waited for Prowitt. As soon as he appeared, we moved in. Simple. Then we sat and waited for him to incriminate himself."

"Wish I'd known. Though I think I'd still have been worried," Chris said thinking worried didn't come close to what he felt. "Becca slipped the gun to me in the car. Along with instructions of when to pull it out. That's why she was all over me in the backseat. What happens now?"

"Cav interrogates them. Prowitt won't talk but you can bet some of his goons will. And if Gray is really a cop? He'll deal."

"A cop." Chris shook his head.

"Yeah. Makes a lot of sense. Hindsight. How Prowitt always knew about witnesses. They'll both get prison time, but in a safe prison. Don't want them to end up like Whitey Bulger or Epstein. Want them to spend a long, long time in prison."

"Whitey Bulger? I mean I know who he is, but what happened to him?"

"Forgot you've been out of the country. He was moved to general population in a new prison and was killed by a fellow inmate. Epstein killed himself, if you believe the reports."

"I can see where Gray and Prowitt might want to cut a deal."

"What did he mean about a key? A wallet?" Annie asked. "There wasn't any wallet in that box. Do you think that man, Anderson, stole it and put it somewhere else?"

"I'm thinking that it was in that box," Kevin said.

"We'd have seen a billfold," Annie said.

"Not if it wasn't leather."

"Well what other kind of wallet is there?" Chris asked.

"Electronic. An electronic key and billfold. That would make sense. None of Prowitt's men appeared to be computer knowledgeable. You saw the flip phones."

"So what difference does that make? And what do you mean electronic?" Chris asked, confused.

Apparently Ryan was also. "Okay Kevin. Tell."

"What he said. About me stealing his gold."

"Yeah. He said you stole a key and a wallet too. A wallet with an address."

"Right. He's digitally ignorant. I don't think he uses computers or the internet. I mean. no one uses a flip phone."

Tricia sighed, patiently. "So?"

"Well. He said I stole his gold," Kevin said as if that explained everything.

Tricia snorted. "Of course, he did. You stole his coins." Then she sobered. "But what does that tell you? Except that he's mixed up?"

"Yeah, Kevin. Give. So the man's not a geek. Most of us aren't," Chris said. "What are we missing?"

Becca nodded, smiled. She understood.

Tricia poked Kevin in the arm. "Give," she ordered.

"It's not coins. Physical coins. Or a leather wallet or billfold. Or a written address. It's a hardware wallet."

"What is a hardware wallet?" Chris asked.

"It's an offline wallet, like a thumb drive. It's where you keep your bitcoins. Or a paper wallet."

"How do you keep bitcoins in a wallet? Paper or otherwise. I thought they were digital." Chris asked again. Was he the only one at the table who didn't understand?

"Yeah. What he said," Tricia said. "I'm confused."

Kevin let out a long sigh. "Okay. Let me see if I can explain in simple terms. You've all heard of bitcoins, right?"

Chris said, "Some sort of internet currency, is all I know."

"It's bitcoins. Digital money," Kevin explained.

"So?"

"Most people don't understand how bitcoins work and obviously Prowitt is one of those or he wouldn't be looking for a physical key or gold coins." Kevin scratched his head, pursed his lips. "Let me dumb it down."

"Please do," Ryan said.

"The wallet keeps track of your balance and all incoming and outgoing transactions. It doesn't actually hold coins. It's digital. You need a digital private key or address to access your wallet. Only the owner has the private key, like your house key or safe deposit key. Get me? It's digital. You need to have that secret number or code or password to access your hardware wallet to spend your coins. There is a second key or public address which other people use to deposit bitcoins into your wallet account. Your wallet generates a new number each time a transaction is made."

"Okay," Tricia said doubtfully.

"I own some, probably we all do," he said. "Let me start with some history. Bitcoins are the modern version of bearer bonds." He looked around the table. "Okay. Ancient history. Bearer bonds were stock certificates which did not identify the buyer. The buyer's only proof that he owned the bonds was that he held them. No ID, no Social Security number. Just hand over the paper bond, collect your money. The owner is anonymous throughout the purchase, holding, and sale of the bonds. They were issued by companies and governments, but became a principle method to hide money laundering, drug, and arms sales so they were outlawed in the U.S. in 1982. In 2008, a Satoshi Nakamoto proposed electronic money, bit coins, to replace bearer bonds.

"Anyone can buy bitcoins, which are digital, Chris. You first open an account with a password and an email address and then buy your coins through PayPal with cash or credit cards. Or get them as payment when you sell something. The digital coins are sent to your email address. Your wallet. The wallet contains a hidden secret phrase called a private key or seed, usually twelve or thirteen non-related words. Like, maybe, *all the birds in water stop sign laugh about bookish metal wars.* This phrase is your signature and it is necessary for transactions. If you lose this phrase, you lose your bitcoins. If some hacker steals your private key and your address, he can withdraw your funds. Understand so far?"

Both Tricia and Chris nodded.

"Some people type the phrase into a Word document and hide that. Your coins are only as safe as that piece of paper. That's a paper wallet. Or you can send it to a piece of hardware and keep it offline. That can look like a thumb drive, some people have really neat ones that look like money clips, which rather defeats the whole purpose of hiding your keys."

"So when Prowitt's thief stole the jewelry from the safe, he didn't steal a wallet or a key," Ryan said, disgusted.

"That would be my guess. Don't know if the thief knew what he had or if he even had it. All we know is what a tortured man admitted to. He might have stolen a physical wallet, but it wouldn't look like a wallet. It can be hardware or paper. Have Cav's tech folks go through the recovered items. It could easily have been overlooked by robbery, homicide. I don't remember seeing anything digital when we found the jewelry, but then I didn't look through all of it."

Ryan went to a corner with his cell and Chris heard him talking to Cav about bitcoins and amending the warrant.

"What's a bit coin worth?" Chris asked. And how many do I own, he wondered.

"Their beginning value in 2008, was .008 cents each. The value fluctuates, generally moving up and today," he said, flapping his hand back and forth, "maybe thirty-thousand dollars."

"No wonder Prowitt wanted that key," Chris said.

"So, it's over," Annie said in relief. "We can go on about our lives." She reached for Chris's hand and he tugged her closer. "We can play vacation."

"I'm not so sure," Becca said.

Ryan pursed his lips. "Saw you mulling something over. What have you got?"

Chris had been watching her, thinking the same thing, but he wasn't expecting her reply.

"Gray? He didn't recognize Tricia. You couldn't see them Ryan, you were outside, but I was watching them. Neither he nor Prowitt paid her any attention. Didn't notice me either. And they should have. Prowitt or Gray should have been threatening her. They weren't. They were threatening Annie."

"Crap. You're right," Ryan said. "I heard that. This isn't over."

"What do you mean those men didn't know me?" Tricia asked.

"She means," Chris said slowly, working it out, "the thugs at the airport knew about you, where you lived, your supposed intimate relationship with Kevin."

"Which even I didn't know," Becca grumbled.

"Right, that was something not even your friends knew," Chris said. "These guys today. Didn't know. And they should have, would have, if it were Prowitt who sent the thugs after Annie and me at the airport."

It was Annie who laid it out slowly. "Those jerks at the airport knew about me. They were going to disfigure me and then go after

Tricia," Annie said slowly. "Prowitt and Gray didn't have a clue. Thought I was just some bimbo. They should have used me, should have used Tricia, as leverage." She shivered.

Becca said, "Right. They only knew what they saw from the overlook. Add to that, they're totally deaf and dumb technologically. I bet they don't even know how to use GPS in their vehicles, let alone use it to follow a car. There is someone else out there after you."

Kevin rubbed a hand up and down Tricia's arm. "How can there be two separate groups of criminals after me, I haven't done anything." He grimaced because it sounded more like a whine then a demand.

"I don't know," Becca said, "but there are. The good news is we have one group in custody and in doing that we broke up a murder syndicate. The other group? When you think back, the threats started about the same time as you found the jewelry, so we assumed it had to do with the jewelry. But maybe the timing was a coincidence. And that means we're back to square one."

"What happens now?" Tricia asked.

Ryan answered. "Nothing changes. You don't go anywhere without backup." He looked over to Annie and Chris. "Any of you."

Annie sighed. "But we have plans."

"Don't care," he said. "Those plans now include an extra person. Wherever you go."

"Well, darn," Annie said. She looked up at Chris. "I'm sorry. This isn't exactly how I planned your furlough."

"Not your fault, sweetheart. And this isn't a furlough. This is forever. I'm not leaving, I'm settling. How long?" he asked.

"Yes, how long?" Kevin repeated. "I have a business to run. Tricia too."

"Don't you work from home?" Becca taunted.

"Well, yeah. Most of the time."

"You don't have any schedule to go out and meet any clients, do you? Show a house?"

"There's an investment property I'm supposed to look at. I guess I could give the account to a buddy. But it's the principle." Kevin agreed grudgingly and looked at Tricia. "How about you?"

"I can do most of mine from here. I can access my main computer from my laptop. Retrieve whatever files I need," Tricia said. "I don't meet with many clients, but I do have one scheduled for tomorrow morning."

"Can you cancel?"

"I'd rather not. She is an older client, wants to, um, do stuff which is covered under client confidentiality." The client was bed-ridden and afraid to put things off another day. Her words to Tricia were, 'I might be dead, dear, and want to amend my will to include trusts for the unborn grandchildren.'

"I do need to bring a notary so we can finalize everything," Tricia added looking at Kevin. "She's your client too. You can notarize. I don't have to call in anyone else."

"Could she be the person who is after you?" Becca asked.

Tricia gave her a sad smile. "No. She's a sweet old lady."

Becca snorted. "Daffy can go with you."

But Tricia shook her head. "This client is a recluse, she isn't going to want strangers in her home, especially a man, for reasons I won't go into. Maybe you, Becca, or Mary Lee? I can tell Mrs. Wimbledon you're my cousin visiting from out of the country. Or maybe that you are my assistant."

"You two work it out," Ryan said. "Let's talk about finding out who this guy is. You searched your files, Kevin. Did you find any names, people you both worked with?"

"Yeah, yeah, yeah. Because we made it a point to partner when we had clients whose needs meshed. Or when I had property one of her clients might be interested in. But none of those people would do this." He flicked his hand.

"You don't know that. Look at Prowitt. Who would think he would come after you? Give those names to Jake. See if he comes up with anything. If he does, his people will follow up. If nothing pops, we meet back here and reevaluate," Ryan said.

"Jake can do that?" Chris asked.

Ryan turned to Becca who considered the question and decided to answer. "Cilla's husband is a partner in a company that does that type of work, background checks. Daffy works for him. I think we mentioned that."

"Oh." Not the background checks. Though he supposed that made sense. You'd want to know who you were protecting—and protecting him from. He'd ask more about that later.

"Will you send Jake the names?" Ryan asked.

"Yeah, I suppose." Not the least bit gracious. He stopped himself. "Sorry. You're right. Didn't mean to give you such a hard time. You're only trying to help. It's just so frustrating, stuck at home. I'll call the guy I swap off with."

"Good. Thank you.

Kevin said, "Jake isn't going to find anything on these people. They are all completely satisfied customers. Completely normal people. And nothing I've done would cause anyone to want to murder me and hurt my friends."

"So, we eliminate them from our suspect list," Ryan said. "Again. You didn't do anything to Prowitt."

"Okay, okay." Kevin pulled out his cell, fiddled with some buttons. "Done."

"Not my field," Chris said. "But what about relatives? If some offspring is disinherited, doesn't get the family vacation home? Or feels gypped? Or you beat someone else out for a piece of property or didn't purchase the piece the guy wanted to unload?"

"Huh," Ryan said. "You bring up good points. How about it, Kevin? Did you look at the real estate deals?'

"Didn't occur to me, but I can do that now."

Ryan's phone rang. "I have you on speaker, Cav."

"Two things," Cav said. "Don't know if they're good or bad.

First, no computers, no laptops, no tablets, no smart phones. No hard drives. Nothing that was electronic was found in the houses."

He paused, disgusted. "Nothing digital was logged in. And we didn't find anything that looked like it could be a billfold. But our tech guys found something when they looked. Might be a thumb drive mixed up with the jewelry. Didn't recognize it at first. I'm quoting our techies now."

"A thumb drive that isn't a thumb drive?" asked Becca. "What? They decided it was a flash drive?"

"Even I know they're the same thing," Cav grumbled.

"Well, when is a thumb drive not a thumb drive?" she asked again.

"When it looks like a pin. A pig pin. A pink diamond pig pin. And it's pass-worded."

"Bring it here, I'll open it. And that means it's a flash drive."

"No way," Cav said.

"Well, do you want to know what's on it or not?"

"Oh, we know what's on it," he said. "Sort of."

"If you can't get it open, how do you know what's on—" She stopped. "Oh."

"Right. Still missing the address, password."

"So we still don't know if it's bitcoins or how many? Is that why Prowitt is so angry, do you think? His guy hid the wallet separate from, whatever? You said he was computer illiterate."

"Yeah. All of them. Computer illiterate. The best answer I have is, seems like the address is hidden somewhere else," Cav responded. He took a breath. "Second, more bad news. Prowitt didn't send the men to the airport. It wasn't his people who attacked Annie and Chris. Or you, earlier, Kevin."

"Yeah, we reached that same conclusion. Kevin is sending the names of clients he and Tricia worked with to Jake. Daffy and Mary Lee are back on the job. We'll keep you posted.

"Do that."

When he hung up, Annie asked, "How long? How long do we have to hide out?"

"How about until we know you're safe?" Becca answered shortly. She looked at Kevin. "Sorry. That tone was uncalled for. I'm sorry. We just don't know how long."

Chris sighed and said, "Well, looking on the bright side, we have this huge house to play in. We can laze by the pool, read in the library, shoot billiards in the game room." He put an extra inflection on the words 'game room' because, Kevin's game room? Well it boggled the mind. For games and activities, it rivaled any of those equipped at his remote locations for the use of twenty or thirty people. Kevin's had two poker tables and one blackjack table. Four slot machines with coins in the trays. Board games piled in the corner. A badminton table. Dart board with electronic score keeper. Table shuffleboard. Pool table. Pool, not billiards, he'd been told. That was why it was a game room, not a billiards room. Game room because of the equipment.

And animal heads on the walls. He'd counted over a dozen deer with antlers. A wild boar. A moose. Bighorn sheep. Two mounted turkeys with their tail feathers spread. He didn't see any rhino or elephant heads. "Parents," Kevin had said by way of explanation. "They liked to hunt and had to do something with the heads. Hunt, travel, and gamble. I remember them most in here. That's why I leave the heads on the wall."

Way over the top. Like the pool patio. He looked around. Painted automatic roll up screens, two giant BBQ grills, two large screen TVs.

"Two grills? Two TVs?" he asked.

"BBQ during the Super Bowl," Kevin explained. "We don't watch TV much. But we watch the Super Bowl. It's an excuse to get together. Those are computer monitors. You know, if you really are interested in a house, I can do an online search for you, talk to my connections. It will keep me busy. Do you need a will or trust?

Tricia can take care of that for you. Maybe a pre-nuptial agreement," Kevin said to get a rise out of Annie.

"I wouldn't make him sign one," she said. "Besides there aren't going to be any nuptials."

Chris's pocket sang 'a e o f b'. He reached in and pulled out his cell as it rang again.

"Yeah?" He listened and then said, "I have some prior commitments. Give me an hour to see if I can shuffle them to another day. Thanks. I'll call you back."

He looked at Annie. "My new boss. He wants me to fly tomorrow. Seems he has a pilot out sick. Is that okay?" he asked her. "I go to work? I just promised you an exciting day of lazing around the pool and unabridged indoor fun. We haven't even started and I'm begging off, but I'd really like to show him I'm a team player and help him out."

"Go. I can entertain myself for a few hours."

With Annie's agreement, he turned to Ryan, "Do you think I can do that? Without a bodyguard? I'd like to do this, but I'll do whatever you suggest."

"Just curious. What if she'd said you couldn't go?" Becca asked.

"There'd be no reason to ask Ryan."

"We can work it out," Ryan said. "They're not sending a sharpshooter. They're up close and personal. Mary Lee can go with Tricia in the morning."

"I can do it," Becca broke in. "I'd like to see this place. Maybe go for a ride?"

"Don't get your hopes up. Might not be room, and even if there is, don't know how my new boss feels about unpaid passengers."

"Whatever. I can sit and wait. Got a book."

He called Roger back. "I can do it. Can I bring a friend, my fiancée? Kind of promised her my afternoon and her cousin wants to come too. The chopper have room?"

"There's room. Pick up, drop off single passengers. Biweekly package pick-up and drop-off. There will be two empty seats. Regular pilot was in a traffic accident. Needs a down day. Be here at one thirty. And, uh, thanks, appreciate it."

"The three of us are going," he told them.

Annie's eyes lit up and she nodded her head enthusiastically. "Oh, that sounds like fun."

"You keep your hands off him while he's flying, Annie," Becca joked.

"Yeah, Annie, no distracting the pilot," Kevin added.

They joked around some and then Kevin went to his office. Ryan and Becca went back to the gatehouse.

"We seem to be on our own," Chris said. "Stay here poolside? Swim. Or billiards? Or your quarters?"

"Not quite ready for the pool yet, how about my quarters?" she said wiggling her eyebrows.

"Race you."

They spent a few hours in her bedroom. In her bed. Their first lovemaking washed away the fear and horror of the day, replacing it with pleasure and passion.

They showered and adjourned to the pool, lazing away the afternoon swimming and necking, sharing a chaise-lounge. "This is like our own private island resort," Chris said. "We didn't need to go to Hawaii. Only thing missing is a cold drink with an orange umbrella."

She slid out of his embrace and went to the kitchen area, opened the refrigerator and took out three bottles. Reached up for glasses. Made sure he was watching as she made their drinks with a sultry smile and a wiggle of hips. He laughed when she popped pink umbrellas in the glasses. She handed him one and he looked at it doubtfully.

"Non-alcoholic. All fruit juice. Try it," she said.

He sniffed first. No alcohol, not that he doubted her. He smelled lemon and pineapple. Gave it a tentative sip. Looked up in surprise. "Good. Very good. Flavor, texture, aftertaste. What's in it?"

"It's very exotic. A family recipe. Lemon, pineapple, a secret something."

He took a long draught, put the glass on the table, and pulled her down, tumbling her under him. "Give," he ordered. "Tell the secret ingredient."

"Do your will with me." She laughed. "I'll never tell."

But his tickles soon turned into something else which was getting serious when a disembodied voice boomed in the air over them. "Ahoy, at the pool."

He bolted upright, nearly tumbling off the lounge chair.

"What the?" he searched the deck. "Where did that come from?"

"Ha, ha!" She giggled. "Kevin. Over the speaker. He has monitors and cameras out here." She pointed in three different directions. "Remember, he recorded everything those men said and gave it to Cav?"

He snapped around frowning at her. "Spying?"

"No," she said with a disgusted frown. "He'd never spy on us. The monitors and speakers are so we can stay in touch even when we're in different rooms. These are good people Chris. Every single one of them. None of them would spy on us."

"Sorry. Sorry. I know. Give me a chance." He kissed her nose. "All right? No insult intended."

Nodding she said, "You're right. I shouldn't have jumped on you. He simply is letting us know that we are about to be interrupted. He doesn't want to walk in on anything and embarrass anyone. When you know them all better, you'll understand. I love you."

Her kiss was interrupted when the door slid open and the Gang trouped in. Kevin stopped short, hesitated. "We gave you a head's up. Didn't you hear?"

"We heard. I'm just finishing up here," Chris said and when

Annie turned red he understood what he had implied. He almost explained but decided that would cause more embarrassment.

Kevin held out a huge platter. "We're grilling."

"What have you got?"

"Chicken and ribs. I'm cooking," Kevin said at the same time Ryan said, "I'm cooking."

The two stared at each other until Ryan said, "I am a guest in your house. Please, kind chef, cook my dinner."

They moved to the kitchen area and Annie took orders for her fruit drink. Non-alcoholic, even though there was a full bar. Maybe it was too early for adult beverages. Chris was happy to see that.

The group told tales about Annie. All had to do with one instance or another when she'd been called upon to defend or protect one of them. All positive, most funny.

"Don't pay attention to them," she told Chris, "they embellish. They were all grown by the time I came here." If not in years, certainly in experience and street smarts.

"Not me," Kevin corrected her, flipping a chicken leg. "You're responsible for how I turned out." He told Chris, "She raised me. My folks were too busy traveling and partying. But they did do one good thing. They hired Annie."

"Oh, bosh. You raised yourself. I just provided some input."

Chris changed the subject asking Becca, "Why did you call Nancy your 'um, Aunt'?"

Conversation stopped. Seemed as if everyone was holding their breath. He could almost feel the air sucked out. The atmosphere had changed to one of tension. He wasn't sure what he had stepped into and quickly amended the question to, "I just never heard of umaunts, is that a kind of cult?"

Tricia gave a small forced laugh, tried to smile. Staring at Becca she said, "My mom's kind of, ah, well not really her aunt. We're not really related. Do you want chicken or ribs?" She held out a half-cooked leg and Chris considered the subject changed.

But Becca said, "Put that thing back on the grill and finish cooking it. It's okay guys. I can do this." And multiple breaths were expelled in relief.

"Tricia and I were best friends when we were very little, and I called her mom Aunt Nancy." She reached for Ryan's hand. "My parents were killed in a car accident and I was shipped off. It wasn't until last year when I was tracking down the person who shot me that we reconnected." She held up her hand. "Lets make that a story for another night around a campfire. Anyhow, I reconnected with Tricia and her mother. So, Nancy is my um-aunt, because she insists I call her aunt, and I'm still getting used to it. I'm not related to her or Tricia by blood any more than I am to any of the other people in this room. None of us are related. But we are all brothers and sisters."

"Too right," Kevin said.

THURSDAY

"You drive, Annie," Becca said. "Same rules. You too Chris."

"I don't get a gun today?" he asked.

"Not yet. I know you're kidding, but you better hope I don't need to slip you one because that will mean we're in deep trouble."

Annie stiffened; he patted her leg. She looked in the rear view. "Becca. Stop that. Behave yourself. I'm scared enough."

"Sorry. I don't really expect trouble, they can't track us, this car is clean. But it doesn't hurt for all of us to be on our guard."

That almost put a damper on his day, but he would be flying, and he would have Annie with him. They went into the office and Pat took him to the long back wall where an aeronautical chart beside a white board showed each chopper and its schedule for the day. A second white board listed the regular runs for the week, each chopper color coded. Landing times, places, and passenger name or type of package pickup. He was surprised they were using something so old fashioned, but Pat explained, "This wall schedule is for me. This is the way we used to do it and I still need the large visual, the whole week at a glance. But we use a software app which you'll find on your phone. I enter the reservations on my cell phone as soon as we make them. The app distributes the update immediately to everyone. I emailed it to you, all you have to do is download it."

She ran through his itinerary for today. "First, you pick up a passenger at this small airfield. Drop him off at the Plover Building, rooftop helipad." She pointed to locations on the map as she spoke. "Next, pick-up another passenger at hanger five at this airstrip." She tapped the map again. "Private hanger. Wait for him. He may be an hour late. We're being compensated for the wait. Have lunch at the employee eatery. They have a gourmet chef; the owner's wife likes to cook and bake."

She moved two steps and pointed again. "Take him to Newark International. After you drop him off, you pick up a package here, just the other side of the airfield boundary road. They'll be expecting you. We pick up his packages every few days. Imported materials for stuffed toys. Guy makes them. Not just any stuffed toys. Handmade, hand stitched, realistic, plush toys. People want toys which look like their pets or a cartoon movie animal and they're willing to pay for it. I've never seen one, but he says his minimum price is fifteen hundred dollars. Who knew? Anyhow, you pick up a container of fabrics and stuffings and deliver it to this location." Again, she pointed to a site. "Pick up his finished toys—they will also be in a container—and deliver them to his warehouse. Here." She pointed. "Warehouse on a loading dock. This is Clinton, used to be Hell's Kitchen."

She handed him the clipboard and thumbed through the sheets one by one. "Your ID, coordinates for each stop, orders for passenger pick-up and drop-off, authorization for package pick-up in the cargo area, and release forms for clients to sign. I put the yellow signature stickers on them for you. The package drop-off documents require a specific signature, none other will be accepted, bring the package back here if you can't get it."

Chris looked over the paperwork and was impressed with the efficiency. But then they had to be. He nodded his understanding. "So if this guy, Robert, isn't there to receive the toys, I bring them here?"

"Right." She waved a hand. "Don't ask me why. That's what he wants. That's what we do."

"Gotcha."

"Chopper's fueled. Safety check, pre-flight inspection, has been done, but I'm sure you want to do one yourself. Go ahead. Complete your safety check, load up your friends, and go."

Chris smiled and walked out to do just that. It was another Bell, a 407GX model built in 2011 with a four-blade rotor which gave it outstanding hover ability. Inside it was equipped with a Helicopter Terrain Avoidance Warning System, a Traffic Information System, Helicopter Synthetic Vision Technology with terrain and obstacle alerting, and a range ring. Everything he'd need for aerial photography. The bulkhead seats in the rear would fold up for the package pickup.

It sold for one point five million used, so, he would always want a Bell. And that was okay. He could fly this one, didn't need to own it. Besides he wanted a wife, a home, kids. Those were his priorities. Attainable priorities. And if his financial advisor approved, he'd own part of Helio soon. A small part, granted.

The women asked endless questions as he made his safety check and he explained each step patiently. Becca stayed alert beside Annie and put her up front in the co-pilot seat. She sat behind, watching everything but continued her questions inside the cockpit wanting each gage explained as he revved up. He made sure they were buckled in, demonstrated seat and air vent adjustment, air sick bags, fire extinguisher, exits and evacuation procedures, and how to work the headsets, before taking off. Only after they were in the air did Annie get a chance to speak.

"This is plush. I expected one of those little bubble guys. You know the ones with the glass all around. I think I might be nervous if I were sitting right on top of a window. But this is nice."

"That's part of the high," he said and laughed. "No pun intended. But sitting on air is an over the top high."

"Your high. I'll take good solid ground, thank you. But I love your uniform. Impressively understated. Long sleeved white shirt with epaulets. Helicopter insignia. Black pants."

"Yeah," Becca said, "he looks like a waiter." And they all laughed because he did look like a waiter.

The first airfield was small, and their passenger was waiting, talking on his Bluetooth. He nodded to them once and then continued talking on his cell during the entire trip. He was still talking as he exited the chopper on top of The Plover building and headed inside.

"Guess he does this a lot. Never even looked up. Could have been riding a bus or a cab," Annie said.

"High priced cab," Becca said.

"Headsets have Bluetooth support for phones," he told them. "No need to end a conversation just because you're in the air."

"I can almost understand," Becca said. "I'm sorry Chris, but this is pretty boring. You know. After the first, well, three minutes, it's all the same. High priced cab."

Chris just shook his head. It takes all types to make up the world. He asked Annie, "You bored?"

"I'm okay. It's interesting."

He snorted. Interesting?

Next, they flew to Maryland and landed at an even smaller airfield. Their passenger was still in the air enroute, so they took advantage of the time and headed for the cafe.

"I don't know about gourmet. Pat must have been kidding," Annie said, looking at the menu. "Grilled cheese? Hamburgers? Scrambled eggs and ham? That's gourmet?"

"Maybe the way they fix them," Becca suggested, surveilling the doors and the customers, watching Annie's back.

"Hamburger for me, and I sure hope it's not gourmet," Chris said. Still on his 'high' even on the ground. He was going to get to fly every day. Every day for as long as he wanted. He was enjoying himself but was sorry neither Annie nor Becca were onboard this high, hah, with him. Becca was bored. And Annie, interested.

Their meal was served. Chris didn't know what the chef did

with his hamburger, but it was excellent, and he got another to go. Both ladies were pleased with their selections. They met the new passenger who told Chris he was a different pilot, which Chris acknowledged. "Started the other day."

The guy threw questions at him the whole trip. Where had he flown before, what were the remote areas like. "I'm a writer," he said. "Always looking for new material, new settings. I'll have to research it. We can talk more on another flight."

Chris set him down at Newark and he walked off after handshakes. "I don't know," Chris said. "A passenger who doesn't talk to you might be easier."

"Yeah, that guy could have been a cop running an interrogation," Becca responded. "Where to now?"

Chris pointed to a sign for package pick-up just outside the boundary road.

"Handy."

"Yeah, imagine Pat planned it that way."

He borrowed a cart to move two packages containing multiple boxes wrapped together in plastic and loaded them in the chopper. The two women stretched their legs staying close.

"Next stop is a spot north of here a few miles east of Montclair." He was going to say something else but stopped because Becca was sniffing the boxes. Eyes squinted, she almost reminded him of a cat as she sniffed all over. She couldn't be that bored, could she?

"Stinks," Becca said.

"Noticed as I loaded them on the utility cart."

"Sure is a lot of fabric and stuffing. Thought you were transporting fabric and filler for stuffed animals."

"Me too. And the guy making toys by hand is making a lot of toys if we're delivering this amount a couple of times a week. He's not making one specialty toy a day with all this stock."

"What makes it a specialty? The number produced? The finished product? The price? Not many people can spend fifteen hundred dollars on a stuffed toy. Wonder what the finished product smells like? Must make a lot of toys for all this fabric. Maybe he makes ten toys a day because he has minions? Minions he doesn't pay? Don't believe it." She was talking to herself. "Check his Facebook page." She pulled out her tablet, mumbling, "Checking, checking, checking. No Facebook page. His own site then. Nope."

She studied the boxes again. "The box doesn't have a return address, just his name and home address."

Chris gave it a look. "And that address is not either of the ones on the waybills," he injected into her mutterings.

She looked up at him. Back at the box. "Interesting."

She leaned over the boxes. "Maybe I can find him by this address." She tapped her tablet some more. "No, doesn't match any physical location. I'll check for specially made toys."

"I'll help, two searchers are better than one," Annie said. "And two different search engines, I got a PC you have a Mac so that will double our efforts."

After a few moments of quiet, Annie said, "Wow. Who knew? There's a huge market for stuffed animals. Some created to look like your pet cat or dog. Lots of dragons and rabbits." She scrolled through the pictures. "Oh, this one is so cute. Look, Becca." Annie turned her screen toward the back seat.

"Yeah, and none of those cost more than a couple of hundred. How can our guy charge so much? Do you see his name anywhere? I don't. How does he get customers if he doesn't advertise?"

"Word of mouth?" Annie suggested.

"I don't like it. Why do these cartons stink? The perfume doesn't belong. If he ordered specialty fabric or filling, believe me it would come odor free. Too many people with allergies. I don't like that they smell."

"I'm sorry, Becca, but we'll be dropping them off soon," Chris reassured her.

"The odor itself doesn't bother me. But it's curious. Let me put it in context. Ryan has a friend in Florida who, well forget the long story. Drug runners used the post office to ship their drugs and they packed them with fragrant soaps to hide the smell from K9 dogs." Becca wrinkled her nose and gave an exaggerated sniff.

"Didn't work, of course. Dogs can sniff the drugs and the soap."

"They can?" Annie asked.

"Oh yeah. They're trained for that. Like if you give them a dish of kibble and hamburger, they'd pick out the meat every time. And I have another question. How many toys does this guy have to make to pay for air delivery? Run the numbers. If the guy makes one a day, that's three for every trip. He sells them for fifteen hundred each, say he clears forty-five hundred. Lets say six animals a week or nine thousand dollars. That's a lot of money. I guess it would pay for air freight. How much a year?"

Chris laughed, watching her gaze at the roof of the chopper.

Annie ran the numbers through her tablet. "A lot."

"But if he just drove them in the back of his car, he'd save a few thou. What kind of sense does it make to transport them by air a few miles? Doesn't make any sense." Becca frowned.

"Owns stock in the chopper company?" Annie asked.

"No," Chris said and they both looked at him. "I did some research. The company is privately held by Roger and Pat. Besides, there would still be fuel and pilot costs."

"Doesn't matter. Fifteen hundred is way out of line for the stuffed animals we saw online, and he has no online presence. A lot of people don't, but they're not running a business. He's not making stuffed animals, or if he is, he's not making enough to use all these supplies and he's not selling them for fifteen hundred dollars."

"All this because it smells like cheap perfume? And you're bored?" Chris asked.

"Yes, exactly. Do we have any idea where this package came from?"

"I don't think so," Chris passed her the clipboard with the

waybills. "You think we're carrying drugs? Strange way to transport them, isn't it? I mean the route. Pick up at Newark, deliver to some random warehouse, where, I might add, we pick up a different package to drop off on a New York City pier."

"If he transports by truck, they have to stop at the inspection points, and they'd be caught. This way he avoids the inspection." Becca scratched under her chin. "No address on the waybill for either transport. Just this name of a person who doesn't exist anywhere online."

They watched her and waited.

Finally she said, "How much time do we have before we have to drop it off?"

"Twenty minutes."

"And from there to the pier?"

He reached for his clipboard and she passed it to him. "Another twenty, twenty-five minutes."

"I'd love for a dog to check out this box. I could open them, but no warrant. Okay. Let me think some more. Damn." She rubbed her jaw again. "You do this twice a week. Well not you, the company. Pick up at that facility outside the airport. So the boxes never get near a dog. I can call ahead and have a dog meet us."

"We're landing at the docks, should be spots to meet your dog team. Whoever you call might have some idea. You really think we have drugs?"

She held up her hand and picked up her phone. "Let me do this. If we can't get a dog today, we'll plan for three days from now."

After some minutes of her talking, then listening, and more talking, she put down her cell. "Not today. But the locals are very interested. We need a dog but they're all busy at the airports. Next trip. And no, I don't think drugs."

"Then why the dog? Why the interest?" Annie asked.

"Not illegal drugs, tobacco. Cigarettes."

"Tobacco? Cigarettes?" Annie frowned. "Why would anyone smuggle tobacco?"

"Money. I don't have the complete statistics, but sales and excise tax on cigarettes in New York City are over five dollars a pack, so a criminal entrepreneur might buy cigarettes in a low tax state like Virginia or Delaware, put a fake tax stamp on them, and resell them in the City."

She leaned forward. "Let's say an entrepreneur can make about, ballpark to keep the math simple, four bucks a pack after cutting in the shop owner. Ten packs in a carton, or four dollars times ten packs is forty dollars per carton. Eight if he is reselling cartons with twenty packs. There're fifty cartons in a case, so forty times fifty cartons is, um, two thousand dollars a case, and that's the low end. You've got—" she said, turning to count cases, "—twenty-four master cases, so twenty-four times two thousand is forty-eight thousand dollars. For this trip. Yeah, he can afford air freight. And the way he's doing it, no dogs or drug enforcement."

Becca flopped back in her seat. "That was exhausting. Let me rework those numbers."

He watched her, head down, index fingers pointing as she redid the math.

"Geeze call it fifty thousand dollars. Wow. And do that every two or three days and pretty soon you are talking some major money. If you import counterfeit cigarettes, the profit is even higher. But I don't think these went through customs. They were probably purchased in the US in a low tax state; Delaware is the closest. But they might have gone to New Mexico and then, even with the shipping, the profit would be higher."

"Never thought of smuggling cigarettes," Annie said.

"Some housewives do it for pin money. Day trip. Pick up four or five cartons of cigarettes around home, drive to the city, sell them. Buy something pretty, go to a show and supper. Go home with a fancy new hat. Buy or sell more than that, you need to register with the DEA."

She paused and grabbed her tablet. "Wonder if we could use a mobile x-ray device."

"You're not letting your imagination get away with you are you, Becca? I mean because you're bored," Chris asked.

"No. This type of cigarette trafficking is a very real crime." She looked at the boxes longingly. "DEA will be all over this. Let's see what we pick up to carry into the city."

"Oh, I found him, Becca," Annie said. "I found the guy. Type in his name but add an s on both first and last. Pictures of his specialty animals, wait. I've seen these two stuffed cats on another site. Let me check. Right. This company, Viahart, mass produces the cats. Um. Kind of cute. Twenty-five dollars. And these other two are specialties from Petsies, marked down now to one-ninety-nine. They're not his toys."

"Website last updated last year." Becca looked up and asked, "Does that mean he's been trafficking over a year? Contact page. Good an email address." Her fingers tapped swiftly. "I'm sending him a request for more information. I want to know if I can request size. I want my orange tiger cat to be larger than life. Okay, that's sent with one of my alias email accounts."

"Be interesting to see how much he charges or if he wiggles out," Chris said.

Her tablet pinged almost immediately. "Auto response. *Specialty cats made for you fifteen hundred to twenty-seven hundred dollars.* That's it. Guess he's weeding out the riffraff. Hmm. No way to respond. You try Annie."

A minute later she said, "Same as you. The request doesn't go anywhere. It's a sham."

"A sham which he could call a coding glitch."

"We're here," Chris said as he circled over a helipad near a large barn on an estate and brought the chopper down.

Two burly guys met him at the pad and offloaded. Put the two offloaded cases on their own cart. Stacked two similar cases in the back and Chris tied them down. "Someone will meet you at the warehouse to offload," one of them said, and they drove off to the barn.

Chris double-checked the strapping, made sure his passengers were still buckled in, and took off.

"Never even gave us a chance to stretch our legs," Becca complained. She sniffed. Leaned closer to the cases and sniffed more. "No smell. In fact, if I can smell anything, I can smell tobacco. Or maybe I just want to smell tobacco. If I had a hand radar gun, I'd know."

Chris laughed. "Or one of those tobacco sniffing dogs."

"I can get them for the next delivery. You can tell me when you're making the next delivery. No one will know you're involved."

"I won't be involved. I'm not working."

Her turn to laugh as she made a point of looking all around full circle, up, around, and then leaned over to look down. "Right. And I'm not here flying with you bored out of my gourd."

"Bored? How can you be bored? This is the best high you can get outside of sex."

"I'll take sex. This flying just doesn't cut it for me. Annie? What about you?"

Chris glanced over, hesitantly, waiting to see if she'd use interesting again.

"Not boring. Interesting. And nowhere close to sex. Sorry Chris. You've always known I'm a feet on the ground girl."

He shook his head. He loved her. Every inch. Even the feet on the ground aspect. Life would be boring if they were the same.

"You know Becca. The schedule is on the wall. You saw it. It will still be there when we get back. Or, when I download the app, I'll have it on my cell."

She frowned. "Be better to have a warrant. Let's see how the drop-off goes."

But that was just as efficient as the one at the barn. Chris barely got out of the bird and two very similar burley guys were offloading after signing with the appropriate signature. They were back in the air and heading home in ten minutes.

"Give me your cell. I'll download the app," Becca said. "Make sure it works."

"You think you have enough for a warrant?"

"No. All supposition. But with a heads up, DEA can be on the lookout for similar packages with similar itineraries."

They flew in silence until they approached Helio when he spoke with someone through his mic and set down gently on the same spot they had taken off from. He revved the engines, turned them off, and silence descended on them.

He pulled off his headset and they followed suit. "I've got a suggestion, Becca."

"What?"

"Why don't I just ask Roger if you can have the schedule? Put our cards on the table."

"If he's in cahoots with the stuffing guy and warns him, the trafficking stops."

"You are such a cop Becca," Annie chided her. "Never want to tell anyone anything. You don't know Roger is involved. You could share one small piece of information."

"Me share? What about you? Keeping this guy a secret for ten years."

"You knew about him."

"Not his name. You didn't share that info."

"That was different. It was personal," Annie shot back.

"Ladies, ladies," Chris said and they both shot him the same angry look.

"We're getting sidetracked. Back to Roger. He might be involved; he might not be. If I'm going to be working here, it would be good to know before I get in too deep." He didn't mention investing in the business. Though prices might be better if the owner went to jail, and Chris had no doubt that's where Roger could end up with Becca on his trail. "And if you're wrong, Becca, I'd feel like I had double crossed a good man. No way to start off a relationship."

Becca rubbed her lip. "Good points. But you'll be out of a job if he's crooked."

"That would be okay. I'll find another. I have other irons in the fire. Think of it this way. If Roger is crooked, when you get the warrant you can include him and the business. Subpoena his books. You can find the stuffing guy through his shipping forms. Look at all his clients. Might get to arrest a whole bunch of people."

"Not me. DEA."

"Right, but you'd have points for a good bust."

She narrowed her eyes at him. "You're conning me."

"A little," he admitted, but it was the best he could come up with and looked to Annie to see if she had a suggestion.

"He's kind of right Becca. Not fair to make him snitch on his new boss."

Becca was listening. From everything he knew about her, he was fairly sure she'd do it his way. "Let me complete my post flight check list and I'll meet the two of you inside."

Becca walked between Annie and the perimeter of the field, looked through the door before letting Annie walk in.

When he got inside, he found everyone around the map table having coffee.

Becca stood and walked over to him. "We'll do this your way. I have name and places and times and his website. He left tracks there. I can find stuffing guy again if Roger warns him And I'll scoop up Helio with Roger."

"Thank you." He walked over to Roger. "Can we talk in your office?" he asked and followed him in.

"My girl is, um, her cousin is a cop. She thinks, no, she is sure, that your stuffed toy client is trafficking contraband."

Roger laughed.

"Cigarettes. Buying them in low tax states, selling them in New York City. All against rules and regulations. She wants to give DEA his next scheduled pick-up date."

Roger stopped laughing. "You're serious? Seriously? What kind of cop? You mean like a security guard or something?"

"Ten years with the sheriff up north, eight of those as a detective. Now working with the FBI. She's serious and I think she might be right. I could give her the schedule, it's on the board and my cell. She could copy it herself. But we both felt I should talk to you first."

"Wait. This is, well, I don't know. You're sure?"

"I am. She is."

"But he showed me his web site. Pictures of his stuffed animals. He wanted to give me one, an, um, a, I don't know a stuffed Siamese cat he said he made."

"Not a real website, and the pictures are copied from other sites. I don't know about the cat, but he didn't make it."

Roger looked down.

"What do you want to do?" Chris asked. "Becca's agreed to leave it up to you."

Roger frowned. "No. Doesn't matter what I decide, I'll always worry. Tell her to copy the schedule. I'm not going to knowingly transport contraband." He sighed. "Bring her in, let's talk." Becca contacted DEA and Cav and together they put a plan into place.

As they headed for the car, Becca said, "This is an exciting life, Chris. And to think I was getting bored."

Chris could only shake his head as they headed home. It was going to be an interesting life with Annie's gang.

"Boring, boring, borrring," Becca complained as soon as she entered the house and walked poolside. "Flying is boring. I don't know how this guy can claim it's exciting. Even when he let me hold the controls. Booorring. Sitting around up there…" She raised her hand, index finger swirling and made a *woop, woop* noise. "Booring."

Chris laughed. "She didn't like it. Been complaining all the way home. Not that I didn't manage to make it interesting." He was still on a high. This was what he wanted to do. Transport passengers, talk to them, learn their stories. Know where all the airfields were, discover their quirks, meet and befriend the personnel. Every day would be a little different, a new adventure. Yes, this was the best job in the world and it was okay that it wasn't Becca's love.

"Wow. Too many negatives for me," Kevin said. "Do you mean you made it interesting."

"He sure did. We caught a crook."

"What happened?" Kevin moved to grab Annie. "Someone go after Annie? Why didn't you say?"

"No. Not me," Annie said muffled in his shoulder. "It wasn't me. I'm fine. Or I would be if I could breathe." She pushed him away an inch. "Becca tell them. It's your story."

"Coffee first. Then story. Because, I'm sorry to say, and even worse than boring, the coffee at Helio is flavored. Today, strawberry raspberry. I had to wash my mouth out after the first sip." She poured herself a full cup, then thought to look around. "Anyone else?"

"Me," Chris said. "Definitely me. Hope I don't have to drink that coffee to keep my job. Though I guess I should be happy to still have a job after what you did."

"What?" Ryan asked, sounding a little disgusted. "Stop teasing and tell."

Becca looked at him and saw the cup of tea and cupcake on the table in front of him. "Cupcake?" she said forgetting Chris's coffee. "You got a cupcake?" She turned to Annie. "When did you make cupcakes?"

Ryan passed her his. "Frozen and thawed, Becca."

Chris got his own coffee and a cup for Annie and brought them to the table. He went back for the basket of cupcakes which was sitting next to the pot then settled in to listen and enjoy while Becca told them her version of the day. She described the day, laying out the facts and her assumptions piece by piece as if giving a report. When she finished she patted Chris on the shoulder. "This guy here is so smart. He convinced Roger to do things the right way and Roger has already talked to DEA and Cav and they worked out a plan on the phone. They'll meet in person tomorrow. Everything out in the open."

Chris added, "I really didn't know which way Roger would jump and was relieved he chose to contact law enforcement. Otherwise, I'd be out of a job before I even officially started."

"Honesty is always good," Ryan agreed.

Chris grimaced and looked at Annie. "In the interest of full disclosure, I have a few items I should mention. Not really secrets, just things I haven't shared. Maybe when I do, you guys will share some of the stories you've been hinting at ever since I arrived."

"Ooh, secrets," Becca cooed. "I love secrets. Give."

Chris couldn't help himself. He laughed. "You are high as a kite."

Ryan joined him in the laughter. "Yep. That's my wife. A good case makes her giddy."

"Tell. You tell one, then Ryan will tell you the story about my um aunt. The aunt part. You have to wait for the rest," Becca said and sat close to Ryan on the loveseat.

"Annie and I have collaborated on a book."

"Book? What do you mean book?" Becca said. "What book?"

"Two books actually. I wrote two books. Non-fiction. One version for the layman, the second version is a textbook. Remote Area Operations and Research."

"Both are science," Annie explained, "but the layman's book has the science wrapped up in humor and excerpts. Very readable."

"And due out next month," Chris said. "What Annie doesn't know, and what she's hearing for the first time, is the pre-publication sales are astronomical."

"Really?" Annie asked with an excited smile. "That's great."

"Yes. And the other new thing, the publisher wants a series—for the layman—on each of the areas I've worked."

Annie jumped up and gave him a hug. "You are so clever."

"You helped. I couldn't have done it without you. And they'll keep us busy," he told her.

"Wow," Becca said. "That is cool. I never met anyone who wrote a book."

Chris smiled at her. "Me either."

"Congratulations," Ryan said.

"Thanks. It's that free time thing again at remote sites. I kept a diary and simply transcribed it. And that leads me to two other reasons I didn't want to lose this job. Penney has been doing due diligence on Helio for me because my long-range plan is to invest in Helio. Invest a portion of my savings and become a partner. With an infusion of funds, they can purchase a larger helicopter and carry more passengers and supplies and hire another pilot. And." He emphasized the 'and', drew it out. "We can work with local educational facilities to train new pilots and mechanics. We add flying lessons and maintenance classes to our offerings in conjunction with the community college. I still do what I love and I become my own boss. Best of both worlds. I fly. Someone else, Roger and his wife, runs the business, does the paperwork. This thing with the stuffing guy shouldn't change any of that." He took a bite of cupcake.

"That's why I'm in the process of setting up two interviews. One with the university to teach as a visiting professor, research and survival in remote areas. Another with the community college for helicopter flying and maintenance programs."

Becca was the first one to speak. "Sheese, Annie, where did you find this guy? He's going to own the world." And she punched Chris in the arm as she said it.

"You don't plan things halfway, do you?" Ryan said.

"Well, you got to understand. We have a lot of down time. Time to work on ideas. I like to be busy. I want a wife and kids. A house with a yard. I needed a way to support them. So, I planned." He smiled encouragement at Annie.

Ryan scratched an eyebrow. "Can you put off the appointments until sometime next month?"

"Yeah. It's the same as the job at Helio. The decision is only waiting for a face to face."

"No." Annie stood. "He's not going to do that. He's not going to put his life on hold because of some kook. I won't let him."

"Annie," Ryan said.

"No. Don't you Annie me." She spun around and pointed a finger at Becca. "You either. We don't know who is after us. We don't know why. We don't know how long he can wait. Will wait."

"We've been through this, Annie," Becca said with infinite patience.

"Don't you try to mollify me, Rebecca Anne Travis. I'm not hiding in this house for who knows how long."

"You need to be reasonable, Annie. We just need a little time to figure out what's going on."

"Be reasonable? You be reasonable. So Chris and I swim and sun, shoot pool and shuffleboard. How long can we do that? Then one day we get cabin fever and go out. Is that guy going to be there? You don't know. I don't know. I'm not waiting. I'm not asking Chris to wait." She sat, crossed her arms over her chest. Pulled back when Chris reached over to calm her.

"No. We have to do something. We can't just sit on our duffs waiting for some unknown person to decide to come after us. I'm tired of hiding. You made a plan and caught Prowitt. Make another plan to flush out this other lowlife. And Kevin? We're not even sure which one of us this creep is after. Does Kevin work from home? Tricia? How Long?"

"She has a point, Becca. We do need to get on with our lives."

Annie stood again. "Chris and I go to town, have lunch, take in a movie. Look at a house." She held a finger up to Chris. "No. I am not ready for us to look for a house. But the creep could see from my GPS that I'm looking for a house. Maybe he'll show up."

She faced Ryan. "Chris doesn't even need to go. I can draw him out. You did it once before without even telling me. You can do it again. You're the expert. Come up with a plan."

It was Becca's turn for anger. "Why do you look at him to plan? I'm your sister."

"That's your response? A complaint about who's in charge?"

"Stop," Chris ordered. "Are you done?"

"No. Maybe. Depends."

"There is no way in the world that I'm letting you volunteer to be a staked goat. Not without me. We either do it together or I tie you to the bed." He paused for a moment, then pulled his mind back from that interesting picture, and faced the others. "She's right you know. And even if she weren't, she's stubborn."

"Uh. Before you go further with that thought," Kevin said.

"What?" Annie asked angrily.

"No one asked about my day."

"How was your day, Kevin?" Becca asked sweetly.

"It went well," he said quickly, "but not so fine for my buddy, the one who went to look over the investment property? He called and said it was a dud. No one was there. The place was locked up. Sign in the window said it was under new ownership and being remodeled to suit renter's needs. He thought my information about it being investment property was curious because he didn't receive a notice himself. He thinks I had the address wrong or accessed old information. I checked my files and he was right. I received the original notice six months ago. The new notice was the same except the date was altered."

"So the guy who is after you, set you up. Wonder if he was waiting for you," Ryan said. "Interesting. He is probably feeling pretty frustrated about now. Real estate. The area where you and Tricia overlap. Who might have received the original notice?" Ryan asked, hoping for a small number.

Kevin shrugged. "It was a specialized sale, so, yeah, it would only go to Realtors in that specialty. But that would still be twenty people. And their offices with employees."

Ryan frowned. "Too many to try to track down. But we can still work with it."

"Okay. Chris and I go house hunting," Annie said.

Becca leaned in her face. "You are not going out without a guard, without a plan."

"You cannot dictate to me. I will go out when I want and where I want.

Chris reached out gentle hands to Annie's shoulders. "Annie."

"No." She shook him off and spun around, her hands fisted. "This is for you, too. We can't live our lives hiding out like this."

He saw the gleam of tears in her eyes, knew she'd be mortified if they fell. Took up her fight. "Okay. We go house hunting."

"I'm not going to let her go out and get beat up or worse. We don't know how far this guy will go. I won't allow it," Becca said softly.

"Becca," Ryan said. "We can work this out. Give me a few minutes."

"Now it's you who is mollifying me," Becca complained.

"No. Just asking you to stand down. I have an idea."

Annie gave him a hopeful look.

"Five minutes," he said. "That is all I am asking."

"I think we need coffee and more of these really good cupcakes," Chris said and fetched the pot to the table and topped off the cups to angry glares from both women. He doctored Annie's with cream and sugar. Passed her a cupcake. Passed another to Becca with her black coffee. And they waited for Ryan.

Chris checked his watch. It had been only four minutes when

Ryan spoke. "Chris and Annie go house hunting. Kevin puts out the word to all his buddies that he is looking for more properties. What Chris? Three bedroom? Four? Acreage? Kevin, you know how to do that."

"Add office space, garage, deck."

"We are not buying a house, Chris," Annie said.

Becca said, "But that leaves Chris and Annie alone. Can he fight? Or will he be in the way?"

"He has a black belt in Brazilian jiu-jitsu, same as Mary Lee."

"Wait. Wait," Chris said. "It may be the same activity as Mary Lee, but I learned it for exercise and balance. Sure, I'm a black belt, but I've never fought except in class."

"But you are trained?" Becca asked.

"Yes."

"The guy has serious moves, Becca. More than held his own at the airport. I was the one who screwed up there," Ryan admitted.

"And we already know he can handle a weapon. And he did do okay at the airport. Better than okay. Still, any plan we make should include one of us with you," Becca said.

"Hey, Becca," Kevin sang. "Yoo-hoo. I'll be with them. And I'm no slouch. I can fight."

Becca nodded. "I guess." She rubbed her side where he'd punched her one day when she'd been out of line. "You can fight. But mostly you just talk your way out of trouble."

Ryan raised his eyebrows and looked about to shake his head when Kevin pushed his argument. "Come on, Ryan. No way are they looking for a house without me. They'll need a Realtor. I'm a Realtor. I know where the properties are, can set up appointments with the owners, and have access to keys if the houses are vacant. They can't just walk into a place cold. Besides," he said pushing his last argument, "think of it. Annie and I will be together for the first time. How can this creep pass that opportunity up?"

"We are not looking for a house," Annie insisted.

"For the trap, you are looking at houses," he said back to her. "You and your fiancé. And since we're looking at houses, we should at least look at what Chris is interested in. I don't think the guy will buy the idea that the two of you are looking for an efficiency."

"He is right," Ryan agreed. "It has to be a house. This guy won't go after you in a condo."

"You'll set it up?" Annie asked hopefully.

Becca looked at Ryan and got a nod. "Yeah. Because you're right. There's no way to know if we can wait him out. But I'm going with them, Ryan. I can be a relative of the buyers, or the interior designer."

Kevin snickered.

"Friend. You can be a friend. That guy knows you live here sometimes," Ryan said. "Okay. The four of you. Maybe Kevin can work out a way for Joey and Mary Lee to go in ahead of you, scope out the places."

But Chris objected. "This guy could know Mary Lee and Joey. Both have been here, and ML took down those guys in the parking lot."

"They both are actors and can change their looks. Even on the fly between houses if needed. We work out the timing, so Mary Lee and Joey enter the properties just ahead of you. Make sure the area is secure. And move on to the next place."

"That could work," Kevin said, "because it's not unusual for the same people to bump into each other when buyers are looking for similar properties. How many houses are you thinking we might need to look at?"

"Three, I think. Maybe five. We don't want to give the guy too many opportunities. And we do it tomorrow. We don't want him to have too much time to plan. He comes for us, we rush him, find out who he is, what his problem is. But we need a way to get the word out. Can you do that, Kevin?"

"Didn't I just finish saying I'm a Realtor? Don't insult me." Kevin rubbed his chin, spoke slowly. "Five. It should be five. Because that's our norm. I have three in inventory. But, and this is perfect, I'll call Charles. Ask him if he has places. He won't. He's not a very good agent, doesn't have any inventory. He dabbles. But he'll spread the word. That's what you want, right? Spread the word through the real estate community? Charles will do it. He'll be so excited to work with me, he'll call everyone to find properties. By morning, everyone will know Annie and I will be looking at houses and will know which houses."

"Not me. I'm not looking for a house. Chris is."

"Four- or five-bedroom, dining room, studio, two bath, fenced yard," Chris said.

"Right. I got that. Um. I can get Charles to show ML and Joey. He's a good guy, if I offer to split the commission, he'll take them. Work off my list. That's not so unusual. What are they? Husband/wife? Boyfriend/girlfriend? What?"

Ryan thought a moment. "Soon to wed. I'll call Joey and ML to give them a heads up. You work out the logistics."

"Thank you," Annie said. "We have to get this guy."

Chris took Annie's hand and added his thanks. "And Kevin can find us a house at the same time."

"I'm not buying a house. House hunting is a cover."

"Okay," he agreed, and they left the room holding hands. He felt Becca watching, heard her whisper, "Make up sex."

"Right," Kevin said. Looked at Tricia and wiggled his eyebrows.

Ryan shook his head at the silliness, pulled out his cell.

Chris led Annie to her rooms, turned her to face him. Put his hands on her shoulders. Backed her into a wall. "You are the bravest person I know. Putting yourself out there. Begging, daring, the guy to come after you. All that, and you're afraid to look for a house to share with me? A home?"

"That's different. And not fair. I can't live my life if I'm afraid to go out, to walk to the mailbox. I have no choice but to put myself out there. And my friends will protect me. I won't really be in danger. They won't let anything happen to me."

"I wish you wouldn't, but I'll be there with you. I'll have your back. If anything happened to you, I'd be lost. You are my rock, my anchor."

"Same goes." Her eyes turned soft. "I'm so lucky. So loved." She pulled him close and kissed him hard.

"Hope you don't thank them the same way you're thanking me."

FRIDAY

They were just finishing breakfast when the cupboard transformed into a smiling bald man. Chris stopped chewing, his mouth full of a bite of French toast. Huh. The cabinet was a monitor. Christ, did Kevin have them all over the house? This must be the same one the gang watched the other day when Gray approached him in the restaurant.

"Morning folks." The bald man spoke with a strong Bronx accent. The wide smile changed to a frown. "You're eating Annie's French toast?" Baldy's complaint sounded like Joey's voice.

Chris raised his fork, waved it under his nose.

"Not fair. How come you didn't invite us for breakfast?" Joey whined.

"Joey," Ryan said patiently, "you and Mary Lee are an insanely in love couple looking for a home. Remember?"

"Yeah, but no one said anything about French toast sliders. With ham," he complained.

"I'll make you some when you catch this guy," Annie promised.

"Just me. Not any of those freeloaders. Maybe me and ML," Joey insisted, appeased.

"Just the two of you," she agreed.

"Okay then," he said with the accent.

"I sent you a list of the houses you'll be going to." Kevin had posted it to everyone. "Gibbs and Daffy drove by them earlier. Charles will meet you at the first house on Walther Road. You do a walk-through. Text us with the all-clear and move to the next house, or, if you see something, give us a warning. We'll go in about ten minutes later. When we're done, we text you. We'll play it loose and work our way through the properties."

Joey was still looking longingly at the food.

"Five properties. We'll hit my three houses first, then the two new properties I received this morning. Keep Jif's mini cameras running." Because there were only five, Joey, ML, Kevin, Becca, and Gibbs each wore one. Annie and Chris would be with Becca and Kevin.

Daffy and Cilla were at the gatehouse watching on the monitors. Cav had been notified of the plan and the itinerary and could keep an eye on the activity on his laptop.

"So the split level on Walther first." Kevin clicked on the realtor's information. "It's a five bedroom. Interesting place. No picture is available. There's a reason for that which you will understand when you see it. Needs a lot of work. And even then, you couldn't salvage it. A tear down in my opinion. The owner has made some disastrous improvements. And neither the land nor the location is worth the asking price."

"Why are we going then?" Chris asked curious.

"Because it's on the list and any number of people expect us to show up. You can bet the word went out, not only that I'm looking, but which properties we're going to today. So, you won't buy that house. Some agents like to show really bad properties first to get their customers to make a full price offer on a better property. I don't do that. It's underhanded and a colossal waste of time. Except today. Today we're going to look at that terribly bad property first."

Annie elbowed Chris. "We are not house hunting. We are trying to trap a man who is harassing us. So it doesn't matter what houses we look at."

"No reason we can't do both, trap the guy and buy a house," Chris told her grabbing her hand. "Are we going to look at houses Annie and I might want?" he asked Kevin.

Kevin snorted. "Yes. The next two. Both near Salem Church. You'll like both of them and will buy one." They watched as Kevin scrolled through the two listings.

"The two houses look the same," Chris said. "Prices are very different. Why is that?"

"You'll see. You'll like them; I guarantee it."

"Okay then, wouldn't want to waste a perfectly good house hunting trip." He wasn't complaining.

"The first house is really nice, but the next one is perfect for the both of you. You'll buy it. Betcha."

Annie frowned. "I am not buying a house."

"Right," Kevin said. "But if you don't like these two places, I'll give you a vacation in Hawaii."

Her frown deepened. Even her own friends were plotting against her. Siding with a man they didn't even know. She glared at Kevin, but he didn't cringe. Smiled sweetly back at her and continued scrolling.

"After you buy that house, you'll go to the last two which were suggested by other firms. Both are five-bedroom. One on the corner of South Old Baltimore Pike and Chapel Street." It was his turn to frown. "I hadn't heard about that one. Five-bedroom, three car garage, nice location, water view. Asking price might be a little high, though the water view could be causing that. How could I not know that was on the market?" he asked almost to himself. "And the last, well, it's kind of a ho hum. Nothing interesting."

They cleared the table and put the dishes in the dishwasher. Tricia would stay behind with Daffy and Cilla. Annie, Chris, and Becca would ride with Kevin. Ryan would follow behind or jump ahead as needed.

Joey texted Annie. *Wait until you see this first house. Gonna love it.* And she laughed out loud when Kevin pulled up in front of the blue split level with the blue fiberglass awning across the front. Chris choked.

"What?" Kevin said looking at them. "You can take down that awning. It's just the owner's method of sheltering the entranceway. Besides you can't judge the inside of the house by the outside."

"I can. That awning is sort of like an early warning system. Warning us away. No wonder there's no picture in your file," Chris said.

Annie swallowed a laugh. "We are not really going to buy a house, Chris. Let's go in."

Chris pressed his lips together. "Yes. We are going to buy a home. Or I am. And this is not it. Blue awning or no blue awning."

"Hey, you might like the inside," Kevin said with a chuckle. "Not a blue awning in sight inside. And it's five bedroom, two and a half baths. As you requested."

Becca stepped out of the front passenger door, looked all around, watched Gibbs park across the street between two other cars. "Interesting neighborhood," she stated and opened the back door for Annie then stayed close to her as they walked up the sidewalk.

Chris gagged when they opened the front door. No blue awnings, but blue walls. Blue furniture.

"You would paint the walls, of course," Kevin said in his realtor voice.

Chris walked through the living room into the kitchen. "Is that a blue refrigerator?" He circled around. "All the appliances are blue. I didn't know they came in that color." He snorted. "The walls are blue wallpaper. The floor is blue tile." He shook his head, walked down the blue hall and opened the first door. A half bath. Blue. Four bedrooms off the hall. All blue, with fake blue wood bureaus. The master, surprisingly, was red and black. The ceiling, red and black squares. As was the master bath.

He stopped and raised his hands. "One more bedroom and bath?"

"Downstairs."

Downstairs was one large room, various shades of neon blue. Floor, walls, ceiling, furniture. Chris tried to keep his eyes shut.

Annie giggled. "I don't think I've ever seen a blue pool table before." She led the way past the pool table to a mini theater. The seating area included three hot neon blue leather lounge chairs separated by deep blue neon console tables with cup holders. She sat in one. "Hard." Raised one tabletop to open a storage area, empty.

Another blue refrigerator in the corner.

"Bet it glows in the dark," Chris said and immediately added, "No, Kevin. Do not turn off the lights." He opened the one door into a blue bedroom, walked through it and opened a second door. The last bathroom. White. "Guess they didn't get to this one yet. And what's with having to go through the bedroom to get to the bathroom?"

"Keep it private. Could always put another doorway in the wall, directly into the bath. But the house is poorly laid out; the rooms are small. It needs paint, remodeling, or teardown. The blue lounge chairs are kind of pretty," Kevin suggested helpfully.

Chris looked at him as if he were crazy. "I will never be able to get this blue out of my head. Let's look at the next house. Can't wait to see what color that will be."

"I step out first, then Kevin, Chris, Annie. I'll walk Annie to the car." Becca spoke into her mic to Ryan, "Everything okay out there?"

"Come on out. Nothing happening."

They filed out and Becca led Annie to the car.

"Hey, Ryan, you see that place?" Becca asked in her mic.

"Twice. Now my eyes feel tinted blue."

Annie was still laughing when they pulled into the driveway of the second house. "Ohh," she said softly as they parked. Chris agreed. This is what he wanted. A white clapboard, two story. Front door centered with four windows either side. Small front grassed yard. No fence.

"Joey says the place is pretty nice. They didn't have time to check out the closets. Let's head in," Becca said.

The front rooms were large and spacious. Not blue. He could see into the kitchen— stainless steel appliances—and out the back window, down a rocky slope....

A train? A thirty-car train? Twenty feet behind the house. Hidden from the street.

"What the heck, Kevin? There's no backyard," he protested. "It's a train track."

"Price is great. Put up a ten-foot wall, place a hedge in front of it, and you can't see it. Hedge will cut back on the noise, too."

Chris was ready to leave. A backyard was an important part of his plan. Somewhere to pitch a ball with his kids. Share a wading pool. Perhaps later a real in-ground pool. Have a BBQ. He snorted. Both Becca and Annie were walking through the rooms, apparently happy with what they saw. He followed, trying to keep the frown off his face because if Annie wanted this house, he would buy this house.

Annie put a hand on his shoulder. "It's okay, Chris. Just because I like the house, doesn't mean I want it. Take the frown off your face and remember we're trying to catch a maniac. We are not buying a house. Even if I were going to buy a house with you, I wouldn't want one with a train track for a backyard. Don't worry."

He relaxed. "Okay. Okay. We're after a lowlife and you don't want this house." Thank goodness.

"Well I like the house, just not the backyard and I don't imagine you could get one without the other."

"But think of all the trains you could watch from your back porch," Becca said. "I mean if you had a back porch."

"You could add on a back porch," Kevin said helpfully.

"And it would be what? Two feet deep?" Chris asked.

Kevin shrugged. Pointed to the left. "Laundry off the back entrance. Want to see upstairs?" Becca and Annie headed up. "Three bedroom, two baths here." He took them on a tour with Chris grudgingly following. Not buying a house with no backyard.

"Look, Chris," Becca exclaimed, "you have a totally unobstructed view from the master bedroom. I bet if you open the window you can hear the train. It probably sounds like surf. And the train whistles. They could be seagulls hollering."

"Very funny." It was, actually.

"The basement is unfinished, but we should take a look. Two bedrooms down there," Kevin said and took them down to view unfinished cement floor and walls. "Heating and cooling are electric."

Chris shook his head, grumbling. "Can't wait to see what you have lined up next. You really make a living off this?" he asked Kevin mockingly as they filed out and back to the car.

"But you liked the house, right? I said you'd like the house."

Chris spotted Gibbs parked down the street and Annie reminded him, "We are not house hunting, Chris. We are hunting a lunatic. Luring out a thug."

"Next house is near Beck's Pond on Salem Church Street. You won't want to look at anything else. This is your house. But since we're hunting a kook, we'll continue looking at houses and head to Baltimore and Chapel. That one came in this morning; I have to admit I didn't know it was on the market. The guy who sent it is a wannabe. Strange he'd get it before me. But, hey. Then we go to the last property. Gibbs and Becca are pretty sure the guy will be lurking near one of those."

Joey texted: *great house nothing suspicious.*

From the front, this third house was very similar to the one they'd just left. This one was built on a side street where the homes were spaced far apart, had front yards, nice size, each with a driveway and attached garage. Yellow clapboard. Wide wraparound porch.

Screened. With rockers and a couple of tables. The front was all windows, separated by white shutters. "Six acres, fenced. The picket fence in front changes to chain link along the side and back. A hundred feet either side of the house. Some woods, some cleared area."

"Oh, it's pretty. I love it. Well I would love it if I were house hunting," Annie said as they walked to the front door. Chris glanced back and saw Gibbs drive right by without slowing down. Curious. He walked over to one of the rockers and sat. Becca sat beside him.

She whispered, "Yeah. He saw something. That car parked across the street. No other cars. Wasn't here when Joey and ML came through. Thought I saw someone duck down when we drove by. Let's go inside, we can check it from the windows."

"Oh, yes, this is perfect," Annie said as she walked into a large open entrance hall. Living room off to the left, dining to the right. Sliding pocket doors to both rooms. Curved stairs toward the back.

Chris stepped into the living room, a great room, high ceiling. Windows went from floor to ceiling. Lots of light. The room occupied the length of the house, front to back, and opened onto a large deck through two double French doors. Beyond that, a pasture with mature trees. No train. He looked left into a large utilitarian kitchen; a breakfast nook set into a curved window. The kitchen took up the rest of the back of the house. New stainless-steel appliances. White walls with a touch of blue trim. Pretty he thought, even after the first house. Wide windows and a French door opened to the back porch. He opened one of the doors and spotted the BBQ pit.

Nodded. Walked through a butler's pantry and into the dining room, full circle. Same windows as the living room. He looked out. The parked car was still there, a shadow in the front seat. No Gibbs.

"Completely remodeled and refurbished a year ago," Kevin pointed out.

"The ell has one bedroom off the stairs here and a full bath." They peeked in. Small but adequate. Had the same view of the backyard. Double doors again opened to the deck.

"Master bedroom?" Chris asked.

"Depends. Let's go upstairs."

Depends?

"Four more bedrooms up here. Two in front."

One looked like the master with a bath. He peeked out the front window. No car. He took a breath. Two could be an office or children's bedrooms. The last bedroom ran along the back wall and had a full bath. And a deck. The French doors again.

"Ohh. How would you decide where to sleep? This is so pretty. Oh, I love it, Chris." She hugged him. He hugged her right back.

"So what is wrong with this place?" he asked Kevin.

"Nothing."

"Come on Kevin. The other two places were bad. What's wrong here?"

"Asking price is steep."

"How steep?"

Kevin told him a figure about one and a half times what he planned to spend.

"Ouch. Can you talk them down?"

Kevin smiled. "Knew you'd want it."

"I have money," Annie said.

"No," Chris said.

"No? What do you mean no?" Annie said in a dangerous tone.

He held up his hand to stop her, but she wasn't waiting.

"Don't you dare try to tell me it's a man's responsibility to buy the house. Don't you dare."

"Wait…"

"That's a bunch of crap, Christopher Nicolles." She moved right into his personal zone, got in his face.

"Uh, oh," Becca said. "First family squabble."

"Um." Was all Chris had a chance to say.

"Right. Um," Annie said right back at him. "You certainly aren't objecting to me sharing the purchase of this house in which you want us to share a life, share children. You surely are not suggesting that I can't share in buying this house."

Chris tried not to laugh. Couldn't stop the smile. "No. My love. I was not suggesting that. I was actually telling Kevin we would not be paying full price, and if he really is any kind of a Realtor, he'll talk the sellers down." He looked around. "Though we could pay full price if Kevin is not as good as advertised. Cause this is the place for me. This is it. Our home, sweetheart. We can buy it together just as you suggested. I'm not proud." He pulled her in.

"Oh, damn. Did I really just do that?"

He tried not to laugh. Didn't succeed.

Becca joined in. "You sure did, Annie. Just demanded that he let you buy this house for both of you to live in and raise your children. And I am never going to let you forget it. The nice thing is, we have your whole rant on tape. You are so busted."

"I don't care," Annie said. "This is perfect. I couldn't even have imagined this. I love it. I want to live here. But I don't want to live here alone. Maybe we could just buy it and hold it for a while."

Becca dragged Kevin away. "Give them some time alone, Kev. Come on. Let's look at that BBQ grill again." Kevin had his phone out to call the owner.

Annie slapped Chris on the chest. "Ooh you make me so mad. You knew I didn't want to buy a house. You knew it. And still you brought me here."

She slapped him again. Harder. And then followed Becca and Kevin to the deck.

"We'll do that new listing, the five-bedroom at Baltimore Pike and Chapel Street," Kevin said having left an offer on the house. "Nice place. Two years old. It has a full butler's pantry off the kitchen like this house. A walk thru to the dining room. I did some quick research, because I didn't know the house was even on the market. The agent who supplied it is a real jerk. Doesn't understand the art of negotiation. Doesn't know how or when to make a reasonable offer. Or accept one. I beat him out whenever I go up against him. Holds a grudge too, poor looser. Tricia had some trouble with him when one of her clients passed away. He wanted to show the deceased's house, but the woman had been my client." Kevin hesitated on these last two words because Becca had turned around abruptly to face him.

"What?" he asked her.

"Is he on your list?"

"Ah, no. Never even thought of him. He's a jerk, not dangerous. Spoiled brat."

"But he knows you and Tricia? He knows you work together?"

"Well, yeah. But he's a jerk, a birdbrain. And lazy."

"Are you getting this Gibbs?" Becca asked, her mic picking up and transmitting the question.

"Running him. This could be it," he warned. "Be careful. I won't be too far away. Neither will Joey and ML."

Kevin's cell beeped. He looked. "Text from Joey. *The five bedroom is locked, no one home.*" His cell rang and he looked again. "Charles. The guy with Joey and ML." He pushed a button to put it on speaker. "Yes, Charles, make a sale?"

"Not yet, and this five-bedroom is locked up tight, no lock box, and I can't reach Gordon."

"I'll give him a try. Um. Don't know what happened. Maybe he didn't get the word you were coming out and he's timed his trip for me. Your clients could look around the outside, then head on to that last property. I'll give you a call if he shows and you can come back." He looked to Becca and she was nodding agreement.

"Okay," Charles replied. "Was thinking that myself. Not surprised. Gordon never was dependable. Don't know how he landed this place. It's prime. And I never heard a whisper it was on the market. How about you? Sale?"

"Maybe. My clients want to see that house you're at now. We'll head over when we wrap up here. Maybe Gordon will show up by then."

"I don't need to see any more houses. This is it," Chris said. He pulled Annie under his arm. "This is ours." He paused. "After you get the asking price down."

Kevin smiled smugly. "Told you I had the house for you."

"We're not here to buy a house," Annie said with a growl, glaring at both Kevin and Chris. "We are baiting a trap, maybe for this Gordon guy. Do you think it could be him, Becca?"

"It could explain why Kevin didn't know that place was on the market. But, could a dimwit, like Kevin says this guy is, come up with a vacant property overnight?"

"Change of plans guys. Joey," Gibbs said, "you have an emergency and have to leave. But I want you to stay nearby. Check the perimeter, the park across the street, wait for Annie and Kevin. ML you need to look through that last property with Charles, just in case our guy is there. If you don't see anything suspicious, come back. I have a gut feeling the action will be at Gordon's five bedroom. Becca? You get that?"

"Yes. I agree. He's going to be at Gordon's house. We'll give Joey ten more minutes to get in position and then head over."

"Be careful."

"Yeah." She reminded Annie, "You stay close to me. Chris stick to Kevin."

Annie swallowed. It was really going to happen, she thought. They were going to find out who was threatening them. She didn't know whether to feel excited or scared. A little of both.

Kevin lightened the mood. "While we wait, I want another look at the BBQ area. That brick pizza oven was interesting."

"What? Kevin," Becca teased, "you going to get one of your own?"

"No. Just looking. When Annie and Chris buy this house, maybe Annie will make pizza."

"Not as long as Amore's is in business," Annie said as the men inspected the oven, inside and out. "And Chris and I are not buying this house. Now, let's go look at that five bedroom." She turned and headed out to the car with Becca close behind.

Kevin whispered, "She wants this house."

"Yes, she does. I'm buying the house, Kevin. Get me a better price."

"Done." They shook hands and Kevin looked longingly at the oven one more time. "Sure do want to see how this oven works. But first we all have to make it through the rest of the day."

And Chris realized he had forgotten. It wasn't just Annie in danger. Kevin was too. Chris had to give him credit for today, putting himself in the line of fire. For his housekeeper. No family. Annie was family and today the Gang was proving it.

Kevin slowed in front of Gordon's property. It had only been a five-minute ride, but it seemed like an hour to Chris. He didn't see any cars parked on the street or in the driveways. Either no one was home, or all the vehicles were in garages. The park across the street was empty. There were two clumps of some kind of flowering bushes he couldn't see behind. A shooter could be there. Or, inside the house. They could be the ones walking into a trap.

"Pretty house, nice neighborhood," Becca said. "Park in the driveway. By the path to the front door and wait."

"I'm in the park across the street," Joey informed them. "It's all clear. Haven't seen anything move in the house."

Becca nodded, reminded them, "I get out first, then Chris, then Kevin, last Annie. Annie and Kevin stay behind us, away from the house." That way, she and Chris would be blocking the two if anyone were in the window. Joey had their back.

At the door, Kevin stooped over and picked up a key. He showed it to Becca and the cameras.

"Wasn't there earlier and I didn't see anyone come by, but it took me a couple of minutes to get here. Guy may be in the house," Joey warned.

"We're going in," Kevin said. "I just got a text from Gordon. He's delayed. Says to go through the house to the kitchen and into the garage first. Something special there for us to see."

He opened the door and hollered, "Yo, Gordon! We're here."

No one answered and he led the way into a small entryway and through an awkward front room with three single glass panel casement windows facing the street. The kitchen was large and open with a counter down the center and what looked like a pantry on the far side. Chris peeked in. It led to a dining room and back to the front of the house.

"What's with all those boxes?" Annie asked. There were eight stacked by the door to the garage.

"Gordon said the owners had packed up personal stuff. The boxes will be moved out next week. Garage through here." Kevin unlocked the door to the garage and reached for the knob. Becca stepped in front of him. "Stop. This Gordon guy makes me nervous. Why isn't he here? He obviously came and dropped off the key. How did he do that without Joey seeing him? He could be in the garage. I go first. Stand back."

She turned the knob and, standing to the side, pushed it open, her hand on her weapon at her back. Chris peeked around her. The lights were on and a quick scan showed one truck parked in the farthest bay from the door. Otherwise the area was empty. No windows. No doors except the three roll-up garage doors, a sheet of plywood braced against the back wall. She nodded and they trooped inside.

"Wow," Kevin said, "that truck looks like an antique."

"Look at the shine on that thing. Must be 1960s, you think?" Chris asked heading over. He felt a need to touch it.

"Got me. Way before my time," Kevin replied.

Becca said, "ML and I saw some classic cars in a case a few

months back. No trucks. But the cars were pristine. ML and one of the guys were really into antiques. Can't tell you how many pictures they took. I'm guessing that's a Ford Ranger."

Annie looked at her in surprise. "You know that?"

Becca laughed. "No. I read the name on the truck. Can't tell you what year though." They gathered around the vehicle.

"You suppose it's a classic?" Annie asked.

"Could be. Don't know. The homeowner leaves it parked over there and has his everyday cars in the first two slots," Chris suggested.

The kitchen door slammed shut and, as one, they jumped away from the truck, spun around and looked back.

"That's not good," Becca said stalking over to pull on the handle. Didn't budge. Chris added his weight. Still didn't budge.

"Overhead doors," he said and headed for the nearest.

The lights went out.

"Really not good," Becca said. "Overheads won't work now."

"There should be a release cord," Chris and Becca said together. He pulled out his cell and turned on the light looking up for the emergency rope pull.

"Should be there," he said pointing. The rope was cut at its source, just a half inch left. He aimed the light at the tracks. They had been hammered tight to the door. Not noticeable unless you were looking right at them. "Tracks are jammed. We're not getting out through these doors."

"Back door," Kevin said looking around. "Should be behind that plywood."

A laugh. It seemed to come from everywhere. Becca flashed her light on a speaker and camera in the corner on the ceiling. She swung around. Found a pair in each corner.

Kevin tugged at the plywood.

"Won't do you any good," a disembodied voice said. "It's screwed and glued onto the wall. Barred grate on the outside, even if you could get through the plywood."

"Gordon? Is that you? Where are you?" Kevin said with a growl.

"Not anywhere you can get to me. Pretty neat, hunh? Owner had the remote cameras and speakers installed so he could listen to music for the two minutes he was in the garage. But they work well for my purposes. I can see you just fine."

Kevin watched Becca check out the piece of plywood and whisper into her mic, "Think he's right, Gibbs. You see? Nailed and glued to the wall."

"What do you want, Gordon?" Kevin asked the camera by the kitchen door.

"You," Gordon said. "Want you and the whore you live with. Both of you are going to pay. I'll get your other bitch later. Work on her at my leisure."

"What are you talking about?" Kevin asked glancing around. Whore? Did he mean Annie? And bitch. Tricia? God, did he mean Tricia?

"You think you're so smart. But we see who's the smart one now. You walked right into my trap. Thought you were so smart. Getting that old biddy to cut me out of the sale. To give you the properties to sell. I was supposed to get those. I'm the one that brought her candy. I'm the one. She was going to retain me, until your bitch talked to her."

Old biddy? "You mean Mrs. Stalten? Tricia's client? Gordon, she'd been Tricia's client for years. Mine also."

"No. Your bitch lied to her. Pushed you and bad mouthed me. Even after I brought the old biddy chocolate."

"Mrs. Stalten can't eat chocolate. She is diabetic, Gordon."

"Don't tell me. Don't you tell me. Think you are so great. I know. You lied to her. The bitch did. You were always there to steal a sale from me. Or a purchase. And then you outbid me on that business corner lot. And later, said I missed a drop-dead date. We'll see who drops dead." And he laughed maniacally.

Gordon had missed the drop-dead date. His contract called for the sale to be cancelled if it didn't go through by the end of the week. Kevin had even called to remind him then given him three days before stepping in. Made the sale.

"Then Mr. Big Realtor blocked three of my sales. My clients deserted me. The other realtors treated me like I was an idiot. All because of you. You strut around as if you're better than me because of all those initials behind your name."

Kevin didn't use those initials. He had earned the designations through on-the-job training, classes, tests. He liked learning. The public mostly didn't have a clue what the initials meant. Everyone in the business knew he had them and when they needed help, they came to him.

Gordon was still ranting. "The old man heard about it. Laughed at me. Called me over here and laughed at me."

"What old man?" Kevin asked.

But Gordon wasn't listening. He continued with his harangue, fuming. Kevin could imagine spittle running out of Gordon's mouth. Could hear it. "He paid. I made him pay. And then I hired those idiots to stalk you in town. You and the whore. Idiots couldn't even take down a useless piece of crap like you. Waste of money. Shoulda known. Found them in a bar, half drunk. Looked big enough, looked tough. I called them. Hired them. Sent them after the whore. Fags. They were supposed to get the bitch too. Useless scum. But now I get payback. No one makes me look like a fool."

No one had, Kevin thought. Gordon had done it all by himself.

"You're going to pay. You and your whore. Then I'll get the bitch. The so-called attorney. Gave you my properties. My sales. Because she was sleeping with you. I'll fix her next. Be easy with you out of the way." He laughed. "Bet you thought the old guy wanted you to sell this house. Bet you did. I fixed the old bastard."

Kevin tried to placate him. "I'm sorry Gordon. Open the door. We'll just leave. I'll drop out of the sale. You can sell the property."

"Nope," Gordon said gleefully. "Can't do that. Can't open the door now. There's no way out for you. 'Fraid there's going to be a fire. Whole house is gonna burn. But it will be worse in the garage. People should know better than to stack gas cans in a truck bed and then park the truck in a garage. So sad. You, burning up there in the garage. Today we see who really is the smart one."

Kevin turned to look at the truck.

"Yep. Left gas cans stacked by the door out there too. And the boxes in the kitchen? More gas cans. I've been stocking up. Ever since I fixed the old geezer." They heard a crash. "Oh, dear. I accidentally knocked one of these cans over and it's leaking under the door and into the garage. Careless of me." The crash was repeated. "Oops. Another can. Spilt gas. All over the floor. Too bad for you." Gordon giggled.

"I smell gasoline," Annie said.

"Me too." Kevin pointed to liquid seeping under the kitchen door.

"Oh-oh, really not good," Becca said.

"Yup. It's gonna be bad. Bought the gas cans last week, filled them up at different stations. Yup. Wonder if those gas cans in the truck will explode. Guess we'll find out."

"You have to let these two people go," Annie said. "They're innocent. They haven't done anything."

"They're with you. Not innocent. Who knows, if the fire company comes quick enough, they might save the house. But not the garage, not you guys. Nope. Not you."

"I'll stay with Kevin," Annie said. "Let Chris and Becca go."

She didn't beg for herself, but for Becca and Chris. She couldn't let them die here. She had insisted they come here to trap a lunatic. She couldn't be responsible for their deaths.

"Gordon? Please," she begged.

Kevin whispered, "Should be a pull-down staircase, in the corner. Goes to the apartment above. Has an exterior exit,"

"Oh, please," Gordon mocked. "Think I can't hear you? I've

lived in this house for a year. You think I wouldn't know about that? Blocked off, rich boy."

Becca and Chris went to look. Both studied the ceiling. "Sealed up," she said out loud and then whispered, "You getting this Gibbs?"

"You lived here?" Kevin asked. Keep him talking.

"Yeah. I lived with the old bastard, had my own suite. Then last week he up and kicks me out. Bastard. Fired me. Because of you. That last sale you stole was the final straw. He fired me. Laughed at me. Said I was useless. I was pouring a whisky and the bottle was in my hand. Couldn't help myself. I slammed it on his head. A couple of times. Well maybe more than two times. After that I bought the gas cans and the gasoline. Planned to burn the body. Took time to gather everything I needed. And then you announce you need another property. I dangle this place out and you walk right into my trap. Too bad for you. Five birds."

"Did you forget, we can call the fire department? The police?"

"Why don't you try?"

Kevin pulled out his cell.

"You see. No signal. I've thought of it all. Bought a jammer."

"Jammers are illegal," Kevin said as he checked his phone.

"Yeah, I know. Told the guys in the store I needed to jam my surgical rooms; cell phone calls were interfering with my equipment in the middle of procedures. Guys were glad to sell me an older model. Go ahead. Try. I already checked it out," Gordon bragged.

Kevin pushed a few buttons. He had four channels on his cell. Only one was jammed. Kevin had added his own apps to his cell, to all the Gangs' phones. No one could jam them. He dialed 911.

"You're making a mistake," he told Gordon.

"Don't tell me what I'm doing," he screamed back.

Kevin raised his hands palms forward. Calming. "I just meant the cops always look at those closest to the victim. Won't they look at you?"

Gordon sniggered. "Old guy has a lot of enemies. Cops will be busy looking at them all. No one knows he told me to leave. Everyone thinks we're buddies. Besides I'm in D.C. At a convention."

"But you're here."

"No. I'm in a dark conference room full of hung-over men looking at computer screens, watching a live online interactive seminar. I just interacted before you walked so naively in here. So, I'm in D.C. interacting."

Becca was talking to Gibbs through the mic. Sending him both video and sound. He'd call the fire department too.

"I'm on my way in," he told Becca. "Can't wait any longer. I don't like the way the conversation is going." The idea of gas made him nervous. Too much could go wrong too quickly. He hurried to the house at the same time Joey moved out of his hiding spot in the park and trotted across the street to Kevin's parked SUV.

Gibbs opened the front door. Choked. The house was thick with the stench of gas fumes. Thought of Becca in the garage. Were the fumes as bad there?

Kevin was talking. "Gordon, they can triangulate where the questions and answers originate."

Gordon snorted. "Right. Sure. You would say that. Gonna get real warm in there. The next sound you hear will be my Bic. Bye. Bye."

"Gordon wait," Annie hollered.

"Stupid whore," the voice gloated. "No way you're getting out a there. You're all going to be crispy critters soon, very soon. Ta ta for now. I have to head back. Got to be in that room when they turn on the lights. No one will ever even know I left."

Gibbs stopped short at the sight of Gordon standing in the middle of the kitchen franticly flicking his lighter. Flicking his lighter. No flame. Fumbling the lighter. Gas was still splashing from the tipped cans and pooling on the kitchen floor around his feet. Spilling under the door. Into the garage.

He drew a breath. Mistake. Fumes. He cleared his throat.

"Gordon," he said gently. "Let me help you."

Gordon started, turned. "Who are you? How did you get in?" he asked, still flicking his lighter.

"I'm here to help. Can I do that for you?" Gibbs asked. Never tell a man in Gordon's condition what to do. Always ask.

Outside, an engine raced. Joey in the SUV. The horn sounded three times in warning, He hollered into his mic, "Get away from the door. Get away from the door." Revved the engine one more time and hit the gas.

Gordon didn't hear.

"Won't light," he said puzzled, looking down at his lighter.

For a moment Gibbs hoped it was out of fluid. "Hey, Gordon," he said. "You really had a good plan. Those people are so terrified they will have nightmares for years. They'll turn and run if someone even says 'Bic'. You sure showed them." Compliment. Distract.

"Yeah. I'm good. Who are you?" he asked again.

A loud crash as the SUV hit the garage door.

"Ned. I'm Ned. You remember me. I work in the yard. Got to hand it to you. That thing with the Bic is over the top." Show respect. Praise. Talk him down.

Gordon straightened up, nodded. "Yeah. It's all going according to plan."

"Wish I'd thought of something like that. That old geezer is nasty. Would've liked to scare him a time or two. Always thought he was so smart. What did he know? I always said you were the smart one. A planner. You sure showed it today."

Was it a Bic? Did Gordon really have a Bic? That could be a good thing. Gibbs hoped it was a Bic and not a Zippo. The Bic flame would extinguish itself if Gordon dropped it. So he would have to hold it very close to the fuel to ignite it and that would not be smart. But a Zippo? You could drop a Zippo and it would still flame. And why was he thinking that? Shook his head at this extraneous thought. Could see now. Wasn't a Bic, but a Zippo. Bad news.

"Hey, you think I could try that once, buddy? Scare 'em? Like you're doing?" Gibbs asked hopefully. Hero worship contained in every word. Admiration.

Gordon looked at the lighter. Thought a moment. "Sure." He began to hand it over, flicked it one more time.

It flamed. "Huh."

Gibbs widened his eyes in amazement. "That's great. Can I try?"

Gordon hesitated, then looked at Gibbs again. Tilted his head. "Wait. I know you. You're the guy stays at Kevin's place." Gordon pulled the lighter back quickly. The movement extinguished the flame.

Gibbs faked a calm he didn't feel. Made his body relax. But couldn't stop his pulse rise. Gordon with a lighter. Becca in the garage. Annie, Kevin. Chris. The fuel must be getting bad. There didn't seem to be anything they could do but wait for Joey to break through the door.

They had backed to the far end of the garage. Chris shouted, "The truck. I can hotwire it." He ran over praying the truck door was unlocked. Opened it. Stepped inside. Pulled out his Buck knife multi tool. Shoved it into the steering column lock and twisted. The plastic cover fell off and three wiring harnesses dropped down.

"How do you know how to do that?" Annie asked.

"Lot of old equipment where I've worked. Lot of lost keys."

Joey yelled into his mic. "I'm going to try again."

In the kitchen, Gibbs put up both hands in a show of calm that he wasn't feeling. "It is okay, Gordon. I'm here to help you. Give me the Bic. I'll make it work."

"Don't tell me what to do. I'm the boss here." Gordon raised his arm, pressed the lever and rolled the gear wheel.

Flame danced.

Gordon waved it around, joyfully. "This says, I'm the boss. This right here." He swung it over the gas cans. "I'm the boss. You do what I say. Or I'm going to drop it." He motioned to the left. "Move. Over there."

Gibbs took two steps further to the side in the kitchen. Gordon smiled.

"Now I'm gonna walk out of here. Don't do anything or this whole place goes up."

Gibbs heard Joey crash into the door and was beginning to hope, but then the engine reversed, and the vehicle squealed back.

Gordon walked to the doorway, keeping the lighter between them. If the guy was crazy enough to drop it the whole kitchen would go up before anyone could get out.

The engine on the SUV revved again. Followed by another crash.

Chris selected one wiring harness. Pulled out the wires, stripped two of them with the multi tool. Touched the two wires together.

The engine roared to life. There was no time to break the lock on the steering. "Stand back. I'm going through the back wall and when I do the roof might come down. Follow me out."

Gordon reached the living room, turned, flung the lighter into a puddle of gas.

The fuel erupted and a wall of flame engulfed the kitchen. Gibbs swiveled, ducked into the pantry ahead of the conflagration, yelling into his mic, "Go Joey. Chris. Go now."

Flames whooshed up and spread like a tsunami across the room. Flames seeped under the door into the garage. Smoke. The crazy had actually done it. Ignited the fuel.

Chris hit the gas, drove straight ahead, into the back wall. Covered his head with his arm. Worried about Gibbs trapped in the burning house.

Gordon screamed. A loud terrified, agonized scream and Gibbs sprinted through the pantry into the dining room chased by the heat and a red haze. He saw Gordon jumping and dancing in the front entranceway in a puddle of gasoline. Howling. Slapping frantically at the flames racing up his legs to his hips. Waist. Jumped to his arm.

Gibbs charged through the room, grabbed Gordon around the waist, and hurtled through the front window. They landed on the deck, Gibbs on his back in broken glass with Gordon on top. He heard the truck crash and hoped Becca was safe.

The truck rammed the wall and stopped. The hood flew up in front of the windshield blinding him. Didn't matter, he couldn't steer with the steering locked. Could only go forward. The engine raced. For a second, Chris was stunned and thought he had failed, but with a crack like thunder, the wall splintered, and the truck crashed through. The hood offered him protection from the hunks of shattered wall. He kept his foot hard on the gas pedal and the truck skidded out of the garage dragging the wrecked wall with it. Sped across the patio and into the swimming pool.

Chris got a little wet but decided it was a good spot for a vehicle full of gasoline. The gas cans in the truck bed were underwater.

And then Kevin was there pulling him out and away from the inferno of the back of the house. They followed Becca and Annie through the side gate and around to the front.

Just in time to witness Gibbs crashing through the window. Then the house exploded and both men were tossed through the rail, off the deck, and onto the lawn. The momentum of the blast rolled Gibbs, bouncing downhill and slammed him onto the sidewalk. Where he lay still.

They raced across the lawn to him. Surrounded him. Chris and Becca knelt down. Checked vitals.

He was breathing. And moving. Just regaining consciousness. Still confused. And blood all over, from a deep gash on his head, and slices from the shattered window glass. It was several minutes before anyone thought to check Gordon and by that time the EMTs had arrived along with the fire department and police. Cav.

When Annie checked her watch, she saw they'd only been in that garage ten minutes, but God, it felt like a month. Chris reached out and touched her. He'd been doing that a lot. Did he blame her?

Becca rode with Ryan in the ambulance. They followed. It was a parade. Joey in Gibbs's truck. Kevin, Annie and Chris in Kevin's slightly battered bullet proof SUV. ML bringing up the rear in her own car. They waited at the hospital while Ryan was X-rayed and sent for a CAT scan. The doctors were concerned about concussion and damage to his lungs from smoke and fuel inhalation. But he was going to be okay. Sore, and bandaged, but okay.

The doctors were keeping Gibbs overnight; Becca was staying with him. Joey was staying long enough to make sure neither one needed anything. He would pick them both up in the morning. They headed home. Kevin drove. ML followed.

Annie sat quietly in the mangled SUV on the ride home. The events of the afternoon a jumble in her mind. The images racing, changing. Not in any order by time or importance. Just popping up and disappearing to be replaced quickly by another.

And around all the images, her guilt. Like the red haze of the fire. Mocking her. Her fault. Her fault. Her fault.

Two scenes stood out in the whole whirling panorama.

The first was Chris driving the truck into the wall. The crash. The front end of the truck folding in on the cab.

The second was a sound. Becca's whispered, 'Ryan'. When the house exploded, and Gibbs was blown off the deck and tossed into the yard to roll downhill. A cry of such love and loss Annie thought she would remember the pain forever.

They played over and over. When she closed her eyes, she saw the crash. Heard Becca's cry.

Her fault. Her fault.

She realized she didn't know what happened to Gordon. Didn't care.

Kevin went with Tricia.

Annie and Chris went to her quarters. She walked to the bedroom window and stood staring out, her arms crossed in front.

"What's wrong?" he asked.

"It's my fault," she said.

He moved in front of her, blocking her view. He'd known something was wrong when she'd stood off by herself in the hospital. She'd been too quiet. And she had him walled off.

"What's your fault?"

"Everything!" She spit it out.

He laid his hands on her shoulders. "What everything?"

She pulled away. Walked across the room to stare out a different window.

"Tell me. What's your fault?"

"That old man dead. His house blown up. Ryan in the hospital. People I love almost dying."

"How could any of that have been your fault? The old man was killed days ago by an obsessive sociopath. A nutjob. He blew up the house. He's responsible. The crazy. Not you."

"But I insisted we go there. I put you all in that house. I put you in danger, just because I didn't want to hide. Or go away."

"Stop it." He strode over to her. Turned her around. Tightened his grip when she tried to break away. "Just stop it."

She glared at him. Then past him. Seeing the truck, the crash. Again.

"Look at me," he ordered. He had to repeat it. "Look at me."

"These people? The ones you say you put in danger? They were in that house because they chose to be there. We chose to be there."

"No. I put them in that garage. In that house. I put Ryan in the hospital."

She would never forget Becca's whispered 'Ryan'. His still body. It had torn at her heart. She wiped tears from her eyes. "Gibbs. He was hurt. Rescuing us."

"That's what he does. And he's all right. You can't blame yourself, honey."

"I do though. I know he did what he had to do. He saved that piece of crap, Gordon. When Ryan went in that house, I thought,

176

'He'll save us'. I didn't even think about him or worry about him getting hurt. Not until Becca whispered his name. Her whisper grabbed my heart. And I was afraid he was dead. I'm to blame for us being trapped in that garage."

"No one is to blame but Gordon. It's on him. He was after us. We were defending ourselves. We put ourselves there. It was our choice. We love you. We want you safe. No way were we going to stand by and let anyone harm you."

"I know. I know. I just wish…" She wiped again with the backs of both hands.

He grabbed a Kleenex and patted her eyes. "Don't wish, sweetheart. You didn't make anyone do anything. We love you. Besides, Gordon was after Kevin, not you. Would you say everything was Kevin's fault?"

"No. No. He didn't do anything."

"Neither did you, sweetheart."

She snatched the Kleenex from him and covered both eyes, nodding.

"You are not responsible for the actions of a sociopath. Neither is Kevin."

She sighed. "What about Prowitt? He's my fault. If I hadn't given that jewelry to Cav, he'd never have come here."

"Well, you got me there."

"What?"

"You are responsible. You found jewelry which was stolen from a murdered couple. You gave it to Kevin and Cav. And because you did that, Cav and Ryan caught a murderer. One who had evaded the law for years. He'd tortured and killed innocent people. You are responsible for his arrest. For saving countless lives if he'd been allowed to continue. You are responsible."

"No, Cav and Ryan did that."

"You made it possible. You. Because of you, an evil man will go to prison for the rest of his life. A dirty cop is in jail. You'd make a good cop. You're Super Woman. Or Wonder Woman."

She buried her head in his shoulder and mumbled, "I love you. You make me feel so good."

He kissed the top of her head. "Love you more." Stroked her. Touched her, unable to keep his hands off her.

They were naked before they made it to the bed.

"I love you," she said later resting her ear on his chest. "I was so afraid that I would never be able to be to say that again. To be with you and listen to your heart. Touch you." She ran her hand softly over his chest. "So strong."

"I love you too." He kissed her head. Love had never felt so good. Held so much meaning.

"Are you lying down?" she asked him.

He smiled. "Yeah, right here under you." He patted her bottom.

She leaned up, looked down at him. "I have a confession to make. I made a decision in that garage. I saw the light, long before the explosion. I saw that if I don't marry you and buy a house, I'll never know what a life with you would be like. I want that. I want to marry you, live with you, raise your kids."

He pulled her tighter and ended her words with a long kiss which escalated.

Much later, with her cheek on his chest she said, "You didn't let me finish. My confession has three parts."

"Okay. Confess. I'm listening." He stroked her.

"It's okay for you to go away. I understand your wanderlust. I'll keep the home fires burning." She smiled at him. Leaned over to kiss him on the lips. "I love you just the way you are, and I want you to be as happy as you make me."

He stroked her cheek. "I'm going to be home with you."

They looked into each other's eyes. She nodded. "Either way." She lay her head back.

"You said three. What's the third confession?"

"Four, I think now."

"Is that good or bad?"

"Good. I want to buy that house. I love that house. I want to live with our family in that house."

"Bravo. How did I get so lucky? Wife, family, home. You are making me a very happy man." The conversation stopped again.

"Good."

"How many now?" he asked.

"How many what?"

"Number of confessions."

"Oh, I thought you meant a different number." And she rubbed her hips against him.

"You're killing me lady."

"But what a way to go. But I'll stop because the fourth confession is serious. A two-parter. Maybe three."

"Okay. I'm listening."

"I want to pay for half our house."

He shook his head. "It's a man's duty to buy the house."

She jabbed him. "No, it's not. It's our house, I pay part." She was up on her elbows again and her eyes were solemn.

"Okay. We can do that. We can make a larger down payment."

"No. We pay cash. Full price."

"Honey we don't have that much money. We can get a mortgage, pay it down."

"No. That's where part four of my confession comes in, or whatever number it is. I have money."

He looked at her doubtfully.

"A lot of money. Enough for us to buy the house and for you to buy Helio outright if that's what you want."

"That would take millions sweetheart."

"I have millions. If you marry me, you will be marrying a multi-millionaire."

For a very long moment Chris's mouth worked. "How would you acquire that much money?"

"The Gang. When they sold their game, Midnight Plus One, they gave me an equal split. I objected. After all, I hadn't done anything. They insisted I was family. Besides I kept the house up and made meals so they could write the game and blah blah blah. After discussion, I convinced them they should give half of mine to Sarah and Michael for their charity. And Penney explained if the money went directly to the charity it wouldn't be taxed. They not only agreed, they each cut their own share in half. The charity is funded in perpetuity."

Again, Chris's jaw worked. "You each voluntarily gave up tens of millions of dollars."

"Yes. For kids to have a safe place. Kids like they were. It was only right."

He worked his mind around that. "Your kids are saints."

"No. They are not saints. They can get into trouble just like everyone else. Probably more than anyone else. They are people, but people with ethics and morals. People with values and a sense of fairness. They had more money than they could ever spend. They gave it where it would help others."

"And they have more money than they can ever spend, but they still work."

"Yes. Money hasn't changed them. Just gives them a cushion to fall back on."

Again he thought it over. "Okay. I like them. I like this view of them. Of you. A rich wife. That's something I never counted on. Don't know if I can marry a wealthy woman."

She slapped him.

"Kidding. Thank you for the offer on Helio, but it's not time to buy yet. I want to learn the business from the ground up. I want to be a flunky. I want to fly people and packages, be a tour guide. I'm sort of like your kids. I want to work. Learn. Have a wife, a home, a family. I love you."

And there was the man she loved. Money didn't make a difference.

The love making this time was long and slow.

SATURDAY

She was getting out of bed when she said, "Gibbs."

"What? What's wrong?" Chris asked half out of bed himself. "Did someone call? Is he okay?"

"He'll be home soon. I'm making breakfast. Bread pudding with rum sauce, sausage, and eggs." She nodded to herself.

"That's his favorite?"

Annie snorted. "No, for him I'll make a fruit smoothie, some dry toast, and tea."

Chris tilted his head. "I don't understand."

"For the Gang. They'll all be here. Becca loves bread pudding. Something for the baby too, I guess."

"Can I help?"

"Set the table, make the coffee."

But they were still getting dressed when Annie said, "Wait."

"What is it?" he asked.

"Something you said yesterday."

"I said a lot yesterday," Chris answered grabbing her.

She pushed away. "Wonder Woman. That's it."

"Yes. You're Wonder Woman."

"No, not me. Pauli. Pauli's Wonder Woman doll had a string necklace and Teddy had a star because he was sheriff."

"Teddy?"

"Arthur's Teddy bear."

Chris had lost track of the conversation. "So?"

"Don't you see? The star. The star was from the jewelry box, the stolen jewelry. It could be the wallet."

"Okay. Okay. Could be. You said the children are in Florida? Can you call your friend? Have her look."

But Annie was already shaking her head. "No. No. Ryan said her cell could be traced and she left it behind. Call him. We need to call Gibbs." She raced for the door, pulling on her shirt. "Kevin. Kevin," she yelled.

Chris snorted because she'd forgotten the sunflower painting which morphed into a communication device. Forgotten that Gibbs was on his way home. He followed her through the house and found everyone in the smaller dining room and was surprised to see Gibbs already home.

Annie ran to Gibbs. "I know where the wallet is. Your son has it."

"My son has it?" he repeated slowly, puzzled. Maybe wondering if he might have a head injury after all? "Prowitt's wallet. How would Colin get the wallet? That's what you are talking about, right?"

"Yes."

Gibbs held up a hand. She watched his face crease as he worked slowly through it. "You think one of your friends took it out of that box?"

"No. No. The children. Pauli. Her Wonder Woman doll had a string necklace. Too big for it. And Teddy had a star. I didn't really notice, so much was going on. But it hit me this morning. I think that star is the key. Holds the key or the wallet. Whatever it is that is missing. I can't keep the terms straight."

"Okay. Let's give Colin a call and ask."

Annie put her hand to her mouth. "Oh, Ryan. I'm so sorry. I should have asked. How are you? Should you be up?"

He laughed. "Fine, Annie. I'm fine."

Cav came in then with a half dozen sacks and started emptying them onto platters. Appeared he'd brought breakfast sliders, pancakes, eggs, bacon, and sausage from three different fast-food chains. The smell of fat and grease was punctuated with a little sweet—fresh hot donuts. Kevin had coffee and hot water for tea, sugar and cream, milk.

Cav brought news too. "Gordon might not make it. Has burns over forty percent of his body. If he does live, he will be in a lot of pain for a long time. The Fire Marshall found the old man's body in the wreckage."

"It's over. Thank goodness," Annie said grabbing Chris's hand.

"More news," Cav continued. "We've backtracked Helios' contraband to a property owned by the same man who owns the helio pad where you switched packages, Chris. And he owns that city dock. DEA has him on their watch list. If he'd been using the airlines or trucks, they'd have had him. The dogs will be waiting on the next trip. DEA will bust the operation tomorrow."

"Good," Chris said as Kevin brought Colin up on the big screen.

"What's up Dad?" Colin asked. "Everything is fine here. The children are having a great time between the beach and zoo."

Gibbs said, "Arthur's Teddy bear is wearing a star. Annie thinks it's the missing bit coin key." He'd kept Colin informed of the status of the cases.

"Well, why don't I just call him in here and we'll check. Arthur, come say hi to Ms. Smallwood."

Arthur came running in clutching his bear.

The bear was not wearing a star.

"Oh, dear, I was so sure," Annie said.

Chris put a comforting arm around her shoulder, pulled her close. "It's okay."

The two ladies came into the room with Colin's daughter and Pauli, all talking at the same time. Pauli clutching her Wonder Woman doll, the star tied around its forehead.

"Pauli?" Annie said. "Can Mr. Gibbs look at your dolly's star?"

She nodded slowly, took the star off the doll and shyly handed it to Colin with a look of pure adoration.

Colin turned it all over. Not a star. A money clip. No hidden wallet.

Annie was deflated a second time. "Oh."

Colin pulled the clip open. Twisted it. Turned the star so they could see. The inside was etched with a series of letters and numbers. The password.

In the silence Chris turned her to face him. "You did it sweetheart. You did it. You are Wonder Woman." And he bent down and kissed her.

"Hey. Hey. No kissing in the dining room," Kevin complained with his arm around Tricia.

"Shut up, Kevin," Becca said. "It's sweet."

"Oh. Ms. Smallwood. You kissed that strange man," Pauli complained.

"Pauli, honey," Annie responded, "you and Arthur found a very valuable piece of jewelry. And we're all excited."

"But you kissed that man," Pauli said.

"Yes, because I'm going to marry him. And you're invited to the wedding. We're going to get married and buy a house."

"Yippee," Becca crowed. "Kevin, go get some champagne and orange juice, and we need more food. Call the rest of The Gang. We're celebrating."

jay gee heath has enjoyed a fun assortment of careers. She began as a teacher, shifted to the National Park Service, prepared tax returns as an Enrolled Agent, and retired as an adjunct professor teaching computer applications. She is a voracious reader and her husband nagged her for years to write a book. Right Talents was her futile attempt to prove him wrong. Now she is hooked on writing and Right Villian is her most recent mystery.

Email the author at jaygeeheath@gmail.com

Visit her webpage at http://www.jaygeeheath.com/

CPSIA information can be obtained
at www.ICGtesting.com
Printed in the USA
BVHW042035020521
606221BV00017B/1581